PRINCESS IN EXILE
QUEENMAKERS SAGA III

BY
BERNADETTE ROWLEY

PRINCESS IN EXILE
Bernadette Rowley
Copyright © 2020 Bernadette Rowley
All rights reserved.

First published 2016 by by Bernadette Rowley
Second publication 2020

ISBN: 978-0-6483105-4-9

This book is a work of fiction. The names, characters, places, dialogue, and incidents are products of the writer's imagination or have been used fictitiously and are not to be construed as real. Any resemblance to persons, living or dead, actual events, locale, or organisations is entirely coincidental.

Printing/manufacturing information for this book may be found on the last page

First Printing, 2016
Second Printing, 2020
2020 Cover Design by Dar Albert
Interior Design by
Business Communications Management bcm-online.com.au

VC:PIE-060120

Acknowledgements

To Louise Cusack for her inspiration and advice over the last
ten years.

To my street team who are always there to support me.

To my husband, Michael, and my sons for their unending love and
support and for sharing in the disappointments and triumphs of
a writing life.

Titles by Bernadette Rowley

(in suggested reading order)

Princess Avenger - Queenmakers Saga I

The Lady's Choice - Queenmakers Saga II

Princess in Exile - Queenmakers Saga III

The Lord and the Mermaid - Queenmakers Saga IV

The Elf King's Lady - Queenmakers Saga V

The Lady and the Pirate - Queenmakers Saga VI

The Master and the Sorceress - Queenmakers Saga VII

Elf Princess Warrior - Queenmakers Saga VIII

Dedication

Dedicated to Pat Garton, my mother and first teacher, and to the memory of Jim Garton, my father, who I miss every day.

TABLE OF CONTENTS

* * *

CHAPTER 1

A forest to the south-west of Brightcastle.

VARD'S breath came in gasps as he held off the sword of his attacker, inches from his scalp. The blade came ever closer as the strength slowly drained from his arms. His vision blurred and the power of the beast trickled back into his limbs as his body surged toward the transformation.

No! He couldn't risk Alecia by shifting now.

Anger ripped through his core at denying his true self. The blade dipped a shade closer and the gleaming eyes of the mercenary flared in triumph. Vard couldn't hold out long now.

As he watched, the triumph in the man's eyes turned to surprise and the pressure against Vard's arms eased. He watched in stunned silence as his attacker slumped to the ground, an arrow jutting from his back. Vard spun to see Alecia on the other side of the clearing, longbow in hand, fingers clutching her abdomen. He crossed to her in a flash.

"What's the matter?" Fear made his voice harsh; fear, and anger that she had revealed herself. "Are you hurt?"

Her violet eyes met his. "I'm not hurt, but as I drew a pain stabbed my stomach. I nearly mis-shot."

"Why didn't you remain hidden?" he said, rubbing her belly.

"I can't stand by and watch you attacked by ten mercenaries and not aid you."

"That's exactly what you should've done," he snapped. *When will she ever learn?* "If you're to stay with me, you must play by my rules."

Her eyes turned stormy. Princess Alecia Zialni had never been adept at following rules, but she wasn't in her safe castle now.

Vard looked at the bodies strewn across the small clearing; ten big men, all Prince Zialni's mercenaries. Alecia's father wouldn't leave them alone until he had his daughter back. He'd hounded them for the last month, since Vard rescued the princess from her imprisonment in Brightcastle. As autumn turned to winter, they had moved south, fighting the men who would take Alecia back to her father and to her betrothed, Lord Giornan Finus. Vard's other mission was to find a mentor who could teach him his Defender heritage. The search had so far proved fruitless, and the enchantment on the amulet that enabled Vard to control his animal transformations had waned. He must return to Brightcastle and Hetty, the witch who could strengthen the talisman. At least he hoped she could do so again.

Vard slumped to the ground at the base of a tree, exhausted. Alecia tossed the bow aside and knelt next to him. "I thought he'd kill you. How could I stand by?"

Her fingers caressed the line of his jaw. He closed his eyes against the surge of love her actions stirred. She kissed the skin below his ear and worked her way along his jaw. If he allowed her to reach his mouth, he'd be lost.

"Enough," he said, ignoring the hurt in her eyes. "We must be on the move. I'll saddle the horses."

Vard left her kneeling there, delicate brows wrinkled in anger. He couldn't let himself love her too deeply when it might end before long. A month ago, he had allowed his love for her to rule his common sense; had dared to believe the strengthened amulet would enable him to control the animal within. Now he knew he'd been foolish. Somewhere safe had to be found for Alecia, and then he would continue alone. He just had to persuade her to stay there. She couldn't go back to Brightcastle and her loveless betrothal to Finus. Vard still couldn't believe the lecherous lord had survived the injuries inflicted by him the night they fled Brightcastle. A blade to the gut should have been fatal.

His brown gelding, Swift, nickered at Vard as he reached its side. It had been truly a miracle to find that one of the mercenaries in the first attack was riding his horse; the horse it had taken him years to train. Swift wasn't at ease with Vard. It feared the wolf side of his nature but tolerated him better than other horses ever had. The horse beside Swift was a sway-backed cart horse with heavy legs and feathery feet. Alecia frowned every time she saw it. Apparently the old grey mare was not the kind of horse a princess would deign to ride. His beautiful lady really did behave like royalty when it came to horses.

He saddled the mounts and led them back to Alecia. She hadn't moved but sat staring at the bodies around her. A frown still marred her brow but nothing could detract from those glorious eyes. She stood as he approached, slinging her bow and quiver over her shoulder. Her long powerful limbs were shown to perfection in the men's breeches she wore, her tiny waist accentuated by the brown tunic. However, Vard longed to see her dressed for court again. It wasn't right for his princess to live rough and dress like a man. Alecia didn't mind, of course, but he did.

They mounted in silence and Vard led the way to a clearing he knew, deeper in the woods, where they could rest the night. In the morning it would be time for decisions, but for now, his tired body required sleep.

* * *

Alecia opened her eyes to the first rays of the sun splashing through the leaves overhead and warming her face. She wrinkled her nose and levered herself up to look around. Vard snored faintly beside her, his face slack in repose. Her heart melted at the vulnerability she saw there. She rarely had the chance to watch him as he slept. He was always up before first light, doing all the menial tasks so he could pretend his woman still enjoyed the luxury of servants.

It was silly of him. She didn't need servants and had never really appreciated them, but Vard had a strange notion that he had dragged her away from the life of privilege, her birthright. What she did need, was him. His rock steady presence and his love were the lifeblood of her existence. If he were taken from her, it would be like losing water or food.

The last month had been hard, she readily admitted. Running in fear, at first on foot and then on horseback, they had been forced to stand and fight several times. Each band of men sent against them was greater in number. So far, Vard had been equal to the challenge, but their luck must run out soon. Alecia didn't want to think of what might happen then. Not only did Vard have to fight the men, but he also had to battle the transformation that threatened to engulf him each time their lives were threatened. Neither of them had suspected how quickly Hetty's enchantment on the amber stone Vard wore, would wane. He used that stone to aid his control.

It could be magically augmented to provide more control of his transformations, especially the bear. Recently, during a fight, Vard had become the bear and it was only Alecia's position up a large tree that had saved her. She stayed up the tree all night until Vard changed back into human form; a fascinating thing to watch.

She flicked a stray piece of hair from Vard's forehead and he awoke, the gold flecks in his green eyes catching a ray of sunlight. His eyes were beautiful. In the beginning, they had frightened her, especially when they turned full golden with anger or arousal. She smiled, remembering her first meeting with Vard when he rescued her in the street outside Hetty's place. Her gut had known he was special, the touch of his skin, like a zap of lightning when it met hers. They were meant for each other. Now if only she could convince him of that.

"Good morning," she said. "How do you feel?"

He stretched and flinched. "Sore and exhausted." His eyes caressed her face, his calloused fingers cupping her cheek. "I'm sorry I was angry last night. It's difficult for you, I know. You should be in your father's palace, not here in a forest with a grubby Defender. You know I'd give anything to make it so."

Alecia frowned. "And you should know that none of that matters, my love."

He flinched at her words, but she'd keep telling him until he believed.

"I don't wish to be anywhere else," she said. "I've accepted you and my lot. I won't leave." Vard's reminder yesterday that she must "play by his rules" made her bite her lip in consternation. When had she ever played by anyone else's rules? She had even defied her father time and again, saving Brightcastle's citizens from his cruel dictates and rescuing Hetty when Prince Zialni ordered her burned at the stake.

He shook his head. "Let's not talk of it then. I've other thoughts on my mind when you lean over me like that. Come here." He pulled her into his arms and kissed her. Alecia's stomach flipped and all other thoughts left her mind for a long time.

CHAPTER 2

VARD lay with his hands behind his head and watched Alecia dress. She did so hurriedly, obviously discomforted by her lover watching. His loins stirred at the sight of her milky flesh, bare legs that seemed too long and large breasts that his fingers itched to touch, that his lips longed to kiss again. No woman had heated his blood as this woman did. Perhaps she was right; they were meant for each other. He allowed his heart to feel love for his princess for a few moments. How wonderful would his life be if he were human, if they could indulge the love that came so naturally for them? But he couldn't bear to be the cause of her death. If he had the choice of how he would lose Alecia, let it be by his ending their relationship rather than by his ending her life. But there might be a way ahead for them yet if he could learn to manage his gift.

He grunted. *Gift!* If the ability to transform into a wolf, bear or hawk could be called a gift, when he couldn't reliably control what animal he became or when? If the fear of losing his human self in the transformation could be tolerated? He had no idea how to control these things. His beloved father hadn't been a Defender, and his grandfather died before he could pass on the secrets of the ancient legion of shape shifters. Oh, Vard had the protective instincts all right, but his lack of control had already caused the death of his cousin, Frel, all those years ago.

If he could discover someone who would guide him, perhaps there was hope for Alecia and him yet. Perhaps they could live a normal life. Hope flared in his heart and he crushed it. He couldn't afford to hope until he knew for sure.

"You know I can't abide you staring at me," Alecia said, her blush deepening as he quirked a brow at her.

"You behave like a wanton hussy in my bed and then protest me looking at you?" He threw back the blankets. Alecia squealed and dashed for a tree. Vard caught her and pulled her against him. Their bodies fit together like two parts of a whole, but he forced that thought away. Her hair smelled of lavender, her lips of mint as their mouths came together in a long soul-steadying kiss.

"I love you," she said, when he pulled back to gaze down at her.

"I know, my princess." Her fingers were twined in the long hair at the back of his neck. He shivered at the feelings her touch aroused. He wanted to pull her back to his blankets and make love to her until she begged him to stop.

She frowned, her eyes disappointed. "You're supposed to return my love, yet you never say it. Why?"

"You know why, Alecia."

"Because you think if you admit it to yourself you won't be able to walk away. And you think if you stay, you'll kill me, when I know what will kill me is your leaving."

His eyes dropped from the passion in her gaze and she pushed her body against his.

"I love you," she said. "Forever. Nothing you do will ever change that. Knowing you as I do, I don't think you could hurt me, even as the bear."

"You don't know me as well as you think, and you don't know the bear. Remember my transformation that night in the castle garden? You felt real fear that I would attack you and the bear in me considered it. I don't know what stayed my claws except that you confused me and there was another target. I can't say what would happen next time. I was very glad you were up that tree for the last transformation."

Vard turned and began to dress, enjoying the feel of her eyes on his body. "I have an idea." He turned to find hope shining in her eyes.

"Will it keep us together?" she asked.

"It's too early to say, but it's worth a try. When I visit Hetty to reset the enchantment on the stone, I'll ask her about a mentor. I don't know why I didn't think of it before."

Alecia flung her arms around his neck again. "Hetty will help, I know she will."

He smiled at her certainty. "We'll travel north and I'll leave you with the Andras until my return." His resolution to leave Alecia faltered at the disappointment in her gaze.

"I don't wish to stay with the Andras. I want to come with you and see Hetty."

"We can't risk it, Alecia. Would you have the last month be for nothing?"

She shuddered. It didn't take much insight to understand that she imagined the attentions of her betrothed.

"I'll stay with Master Andra and his wife, but promise you'll return."

Vard made the pledge knowing he wouldn't hesitate to break it if it would protect his love.

Night lay over Brightcastle town as the hawk soared high above the rooftops. A burning need drove the handsome bird toward a double-story shack that lay in an alley back from the main street. The hawk's keen eye saw much, even in the gloom. A rat scuttled across the cobbles of the main street and a black cat skulked around the corner of a tavern. A figure in dark clothes ran lightly across the rooftops to disappear into the window of an adjacent dwelling. Finally, the bird plummeted from the sky and landed on the rim of a rain barrel at the back of the house.

Vard felt his feathers shrink and his limbs lengthen as the transformation took hold. Slowly, his thought turned from flight and a juicy rabbit to the matter at hand. Finally, he sat on the rain barrel and spat a feather from his mouth. He ran his fingers through his hair, trying to focus on the purpose of his visit. If the witch knew anything, she must share her secrets.

He stood on the rim of the barrel and leapt to grab the windowsill above him. The timber groaned with his weight but held. He pushed open the window and pulled himself through, dropping to the floor just as something brushed past his ear.

"One step closer and the next will be through your heart," a voice rasped.

Despite himself, Vard shivered. The old woman had more than enough tricks to keep her safe from most intruders.

"Hetty, it's I, Vard Anton."

There was a rustle and a lamp flared beside the bed. Vard threw his arm up to shield his eyes from the sudden bright light. Hetty stood by the bed, her black eyes boring into him, wild gray hair even more untidy than usual.

"I thought never to see you again, changeling. I suppose you need my help." Sudden alarm exposed the whites of her eyes. "Is the princess well?"

"Alecia is well, but the amulet has failed."

The witch took a step forward. "I wondered how long my enchantment would last. You're certain the princess is unharmed?"

"She's fine, but you must know that."

"I know nothing of the sort, Captain. My scrying has shown Alecia in danger from mercenaries on almost a daily basis this last month. I might have known you wouldn't be able to keep her safe."

He shook his head impatiently. "Would you cease your badgering? I need your help."

"As always! How it must irk you to come crawling to me when something needs fixing."

He ground his teeth. No one could get under his skin as Hetty could. "I'd be grateful if you could place another spell on my amulet," he said, gripping the stone to aid control of his temper.

Hetty considered him. Vard thought he saw a spark of compassion in her eyes.

"Come to the kitchen and I'll brew you some tea. You look hungry." She motioned for him to precede her through the door and down the narrow stairs to the floor below. Hetty swept by him when they reached the door to the kitchen. "Stay here, I must close the curtain," she said as she disappeared into the room.

Vard waited in the hall until Hetty called him through.

"You took a risk coming here, for you and for me. So far, I've managed to escape the notice of the prince. If you're seen hanging around here, someone will come asking questions."

"I was careful." He wasn't about to explain all his secrets to the witch. "What news of Finus?" He swung his cloak off and laid it across a chair.

Hetty crossed to the fire, laid more logs and placed the kettle on a hook over the flames. "He still lives, though my scrying shows a very ill man. Official word is that he will make a full recovery, but I have my doubts."

Vard nodded. It was as he thought. "And what other news?"

"The prince searches for a bride." The witch placed two cups and saucers on the sturdy wooden table and cut thick slabs of bread. "He has four young women at the castle, and it's said he'll choose a wife from among them."

Vard stared. "Alecia won't be pleased to hear that. As much as she's angry with her father, she won't want him to replace her mother." He doubted he'd even mention the news to Alecia.

"You could well be right, Captain, but I don't think the princess can influence anything her father decides. She couldn't do it when she was here and she most certainly can do nothing in exile."

Vard's anger simmered at the censure in Hetty's voice. He leaned on the table. "What would you suggest? That Alecia return to sort matters out?"

An uncomfortable silence stretched between them as they stared at each other. Finally Hetty looked away. "As much as I'd like her away from you and the danger you pose," she said, "her return now wouldn't be wise. The kingdom will have to manage without her for the time being." She moved to the fireplace and busied herself with brewing the tea.

Vard sat and buttered himself a piece of bread, smearing it with honey. It had been a long time since he had eaten fresh baked bread. Hetty poured two cups of tea then held her hand out to Vard.

"Pass me your amulet."

He unthreaded the amber stone from the leather cord around his neck and handed it to her. Hetty placed the stone on the kitchen table and turned to the shelves behind her, selecting four jars. She removed one item from each. Vard didn't need to read the labels to know what she chose: claw of bear, feather of hawk, tooth of wolf, and skin of human. They were parts of all the creatures that resided within him. Goddess help him, but it was the sad truth, the curse of his birthright.

Distracted by morose thoughts of the reality of his existence, Vard didn't notice Hetty's hand pause over the jar of human skin and then reach for his head.

"Ouch!" he said, as she jerked a hunk of hair from his scalp. "What are you about?"

Hetty barely spared him a glance. "If you want my help you'll mind your manners. Last time I used human skin. This time I'll use your hair. Just thank the Goddess I don't require anything more painful, yet."

Was that a smirk he could see beneath the old witch's whiskers? "Don't try my patience, woman," he growled.

Hetty snorted. She gathered her ingredients and the amber stone, in her palms. She closed her eyes and began chanting a spell under her breath. Orange fumes swirled from between her fingers, slowly turning to red as the chanting continued. The smoke swirled into an upward spiral and oozed across the ceiling. Acrid fumes burned the back of Vard's throat and made his eyes water. He gulped the rest of his tea to wash the unpleasantness from his mouth. Hetty seemed not to be affected at all. She grinned as he mopped his tears with a kitchen towel, and held out the stone for his inspection. As in the past, the talisman had turned to crimson, but now he spied in its depths the forms of the ingredients Hetty had used in her spell.

"Will fusing the animal elements make it stronger, or last longer?" Vard asked.

"I can't say," Hetty said. "It could make it weaker."

Frustration boiled up at not knowing. To avoid speaking the harsh words that threatened to spill from his mouth, Vard took the stone and fastened it back around his throat. He gripped the talisman in his left hand and focused on the composure he needed. Instant calm enveloped him.

"Thank you," he said.

"Never mind that," she said, "tell me about the princess. I want to know how she is."

"Alecia is as well as can be expected considering she is living rough," he said, his voice harsh. "She is as brave as a lion, but we are pursued by more of her father's men every day and I fear it won't be long until we succumb. She insists on staying with me but the last month has taught me the folly in this. You once suggested I search for someone who could help me master my transformations. I thought maybe you knew of someone?"

"As it happens, I might know something."

Vard stiffened, every nerve alert. "What is it?"

"I've heard of a powerful wizard said to have the ability to transform into other shapes. The tales come from several sources, which might mean there is some truth to them. You may find this sorcerer in Amitania if the rumors are to be believed."

"Amitania," Vard said. "That's the lost metropolis that lies to the north of here."

"It is," Hetty said, "but beware. I've heard fell things about the wizard and the ruined city. It may not be safe to enter there, and your welcome couldn't be assured."

"I can't afford to ignore this chance, Hetty, but thank you for the warning."

"It may be just stories with no substance."

"I think not," he said. "Alecia has had dark dreams of a sinister man whose abode is a ruined city. Perhaps they are premonitions."

Hetty's brows drew down and she was silent for a moment. "She has often spoken of vivid dreams but I dismissed them as products of her overactive imagination."

"Alecia doesn't suffer from wild fancies," he snapped.

"My, my," Hetty said. "You *have* grown attached to the princess, haven't you, changeling?

Vard fought his temper. "It's none of your concern."

"You're not happy about your love for Alecia. You fight it every day. Am I right?"

"I can do nothing about my feelings for her. What I *can* do is keep her safe, from myself, and from her father's men and Finus. That I will do if I have to lose my life in the process."

"If I know the girl, she has given her heart and soul to you. See that you respect it."

"As I said, it's none of your concern."

"If anything happens to her, I'll make it my business to track you down and make you sorry. Remember that."

Vard stared at the witch for a long moment and then nodded. There weren't many who could stare him out like that. He folded a slab of bread and honey in his hand. Hetty stood and wrapped the rest of the loaf in a linen cloth and handed it to him. "For the princess," she said. "Tell her I said 'hello'."

"Thank you." He followed Hetty out of the kitchen and down the hallway to the back door. She opened it and let him out without another word. He crouched in the lee of the rain barrel, shoved the bread in the pocket of his cloak and gripped the amber stone at his throat. The image of the hawk slowly formed in his mind, bone by bone, feather by feather, until it took on a life of its own. His body changed into the black and gold bird. It pushed off with powerful talons and surged into the night sky, potent strokes of its magnificent wings carrying it steadily westward. Perhaps there would be a juicy rabbit on the return flight.

CHAPTER 3

ALECIA maintained a vigil for a full day and night while Mistress Andra kept her company. She hadn't told the farm wife where Vard was going. After all, the trip to Brightcastle and back should take eight days by horseback, not the mere sixteen hours Vard had estimated it would take to fly. Alecia was glad of the company, as it helped her to occasionally forget the risks her beloved was taking. The hawk was his most vulnerable form, for obvious reasons. One well-placed arrow and his life would be over.

"Don't be concerned for the captain, Princess," her hostess said, a smile creasing the corners of her mouth. "He can look after himself. It's you I'm concerned about. You're pale. Are you ill?"

"Oh, no, Mistress, just the odd twinge and some nausea. I do get tired, but it's this sleeping rough that does it." Alecia's face grew hot as she remembered another reason she often lost sleep.

The sharp eyes of the farm wife didn't miss the blush. "You take care or you'll be with child before long, then see how well you do on the road. Have you been taking your mugwort and parsley tea each morning?"

Alecia's stomach flipped and bile rose in her throat. She stared at Mistress Andra, her mouth dry and her hand on her stomach. The nausea and the cramps. . . she could already be with child! How could she be so stupid?

"How long have you been on the road, Princess?"

Alecia counted back. It was hard to remember exactly. "A little over one month, Mistress, and I have not had a bleed in all that time. It's weeks overdue and I never thought!"

Mistress Andra stood and came to rest her hand on Alecia's shoulder. "It's not the end of the world, Princess. You have a good man with you and he'll see you right. We'll always take you in if you need a home. I know what you did for us."

Alecia frowned. "What do you mean?"

"It was you who killed the mercenaries that murdered my boy."

Alecia noted her failure to use her son's name. *Too painful.* Alecia still flinched every time she remembered her friend lay cold in a grave. He had been so much a part of her life. Not just her companion but her first love, albeit an innocent one. Her musings were cut short as Mistress Andra continued.

"All but one, I heard. You don't know what comfort that gives Thom and me to know that our son's death was avenged."

"Who told you?"

"It was the prince himself. Rode out here and told us the whole story. Of how the men overstepped their bounds and how you cut them down one by one. He was looking for you and thought you might be with us. He assured me that the remaining mercenary would be crucified and gave me a purse of gold. I truly believe he was trying to make amends for our loss. The prince is out of his mind with worry and grief over losing you."

Alecia couldn't believe what she heard. "When did he do this?"

"Three weeks ago, near enough. I thanked him and he went on his way. Princess, can I tell him I've seen you?"

"No! He may have done the right thing by you finally but he doesn't deserve the name 'father'." Alecia's chest ached with the pain of her father's betrayal all over again. "You don't know how I've been treated by him. Father locked me in a dungeon and wanted to marry me off. Lord Finus is so old and he touched me. . ." Her voice ended in a sob and Mistress Andra patted her shoulder.

"No need to tell me, Princess. It's all over now. I won't go telling your father anything. Dry your eyes." She handed Alecia a cloth. "So you haven't been taking the tea then?"

Alecia shook her head.

"It will be too early for me to tell by feel if you're with child, but you'll know soon enough. You must take care of yourself."

Alecia laid her hands across her abdomen, imagining the new life that could be growing within her. *Vard's child.* Through the fear, a small spark of excitement flared. She couldn't be sad about having his child, but she couldn't tell him, or he would certainly leave her behind. He wouldn't take the risk of hurting her or the child by living rough. "Don't say anything to the captain, Mistress."

"As you wish, Princess. Now dry your eyes, he'll be back soon." Mistress Andra glanced out the window and Alecia thought she looked worried. "It's nearly dawn."

A faint rim of light through the window did indeed herald the new day. Alecia's pulse quickened. She had expected Vard back before this. "I wonder what can have kept him. Do you think he's safe?" Perhaps a fat rabbit had crossed his path on the flight? She knew he wouldn't be able to pass up the chance of a meal as the hawk. The thought of fresh meat made her ill.

There was a scrape at the door and then a knock. Mistress Andra flew to the door and opened it a crack. "Welcome back, Captain Anton." She cast a look at Alecia. "We were just talking of you."

He looked tired. Shadows lay deep beneath his eyes and his shoulder-length black curls were mussed by the wind. The golden flecks of his eyes stood out more than usual.

As Alecia stood, dizziness swept over her and she grabbed for the back of a chair to support herself. Vard reached her in a flash and helped her back into her seat. "Sit still, Alecia, and the mistress will fetch you tea and honey." His gaze ran over her, penetrating despite his weariness. "Are you well?"

Her heart melted at the warmth in his eyes. "You took longer than I thought."

"You need not have worried," he said, as Mistress Andra placed two warm mugs of steaming tea on the table. He glanced up at the woman.

"She has been poorly of late, Mistress. Is there anything you can give her? A tonic perhaps?"

"I'm no wise woman, Captain, but the princess needs rest and good food. She shouldn't be on the road."

Alecia glared at her. As if Vard needed any reminders that her life had not been ideal for the past month!

"Rest and good food she shall have, Mistress, at least today. Is there a room where we can bed down? Once we've slept, we'll break our fast and leave your home in peace. We have many miles to travel before our journey is at an end."

Mistress Andra showed them to a small room at the back of the house. A fire crackled in the tiny fireplace and the bed appeared freshly made. "Sleep well," she said and closed the door behind her.

Vard tucked Alecia up in bed with her sweet tea and handed her the end of bread that Hetty had provided. "From Hetty," he said.

She placed the bread to her nose and breathed deeply. "She always did bake the best bread," she said. "Is Hetty well? Did she have any news?"

"Quite well. Actually, I would say unchanged except she is less fearful of me than ever before. She says she has attracted no attention from your father."

Alecia released breath she hadn't realized she was holding. "That's good. I was worried for her. Father hates witches and he tried once already to kill Hetty. She was my first rescue."

Vard smiled. "No wonder she loves you so."

"She doesn't love me, she tolerates my little whims. I would say fondness and obligation drive Hetty where I'm concerned."

"How can you be so blind? Hetty loves you like a granddaughter."

"But she's always so cross with me."

"She'd do anything for you. Even to laying down her life. As would I," he added softly, caressing her face with the back of his fingers. "Hetty has told me of a wizard who might help me. He resides in Amitania. I intend to travel there and discover if the rumors are true."

"Amitania," Alecia whispered. "The lost city of Amitania . . ." A vision of dark dreams flashed into her mind. "My dream! This wizard could be the man in my dreams." She shuddered. "If it is he, I don't like your chances of help. I can never see his face, but his form fills me with dread."

"It's nothing to dwell on, dearest. It's time to lay your head on the pillow and get some rest." So saying, Vard removed his boots and lay down beside Alecia in the cramped bed. She turned on her side and pushed her back against his hard body, grateful for the warmth. He seemed content to snuggle there with her, and for that she was grateful. She wouldn't couple with him again until she had confirmation of her pregnancy. If it became clear she was not with child, she could begin taking the tea, for she really didn't wish to be burdened with a baby when her life was so uncertain.

Alecia closed her eyes and was soon asleep.

* * *

Vard awoke hours later with the sun sliding its way down the sky. It was only two hours until dark. He reached out and woke Alecia. She opened her eyes and sought his face and his heart lurched. She looked so tired and it was his fault. Never mind he had rescued her from an impossible situation, he should be able to provide for her. This was no way for anyone to live.

She reached out and cupped his face in her fingers. "Don't fret, my love, I'm well."

"Am I that transparent?" he said, frowning at her. It was not always so. If he was losing his protective mechanisms, they had no hope.

"You're still fierce and aloof enough for two men, Vard. You forget I know you well and you'd be stone not to allow me past your defenses."

A worm of unease squirmed in his gut. He wasn't comfortable with his feelings for Alecia. He feared the changes taking place within his heart because they would leave him vulnerable. He couldn't afford a weakness that would threaten Alecia's life, but without her, his life would be mere existence. If he could learn his gift and control it, perhaps they had a chance.

He leant forward and kissed her on the lips, a light feather touch that left him wanting so much more. He pulled away and rose, drawing on his boots and gathering his weapons. "I'll prepare us a meal while you ready yourself, my love."

They feasted on warm bread and thick goat stew washed down with wine. Mistress Andra pushed a lumpy sack at Vard as they prepared to leave. "Here are some things for the road, including a tea I told the princess about, for medicinal purposes." She cast her eyes at Alecia and lowered her voice. "I wish you'd stay another night, Captain. She's tired."

"Thank you, Mistress Andra. You've been more generous than we could have wished for. We won't impose on your kindness for a moment longer. I'll care for the princess."

"See that you do."

Vard stared at the woman and her eyes dropped under his gaze.

"Don't pester the man, Dana, we've done what we can." Master Andra turned to Vard. "May the Goddess protect you and the princess, Captain. You're always welcome here."

Alecia paid her respects and they rode into the first flakes of a snow fall. As Vard looked back, Mistress Andra was wringing her hands in the doorway, her husband patting her shoulder. His eyes shifted to Alecia, who already had a hand on her stomach as though she suffered more cramps.

A sudden gust of wind brought a flurry of snowflakes that spattered his face with icy sprinkles. He almost turned back to the warmth of the farmhouse. "Perhaps you should stay with the Andras, Alecia. The weather doesn't look kind."

"I told you I would die without you, beloved. Don't worry. I'm strong as an ox." She flinched again as her horse leapt over a rock.

"Did the mistress shed any light on those cramps?"

She frowned. "I'll be fine. Let that be the end of the conversation for this day. I'm not going back to the farmhouse."

When she got that look, there was no budging her. She could be stubborn, a trait only matched by her toughness. In all the days they had been together, he had never heard one complaint from her. Perhaps she feared that he'd set her aside at the slightest indication of discomfort, but more likely she was honest when she assured him that his company was all she required. That couldn't last. Winter hadn't yet set in and already they had the first snows. He must find them shelter before the weather turned really nasty. Amitania might offer the sanctuary they required, but Vard harbored a sense of foreboding when he contemplated the place. He hoped it was just his innate Defender wariness.

They traveled through the building storm until near dark, when Vard found a small clearing in the trees. They threaded evergreen pine branches through the trees to make a windbreak and tied the horses to one side of the small space. They spread their packs on the other side. The snow stopped soon after their preparations were complete.

"Now," Alecia said, "this is really quite cozy."

Vard smiled to himself as he made a roaring fire with the wood they had carried with them from the farmhouse. Alecia made tea, and they ate more fresh bread and olives and a rich goat's cheese. He delighted in the rosy cheeks of his princess as she sat by the fire with him. Her company was pure enjoyment if he forgot their situation. That made him wonder when they could expect to be accosted by the next band of the prince's mercenaries.

CHAPTER 4

ALECIA dozed in the saddle as she rode. She had lost track of the days since they left the Andras but it must have been close to a week – a week of sudden snowstorms and cold extremities. A week where she felt increasingly ill, her stomach churning for most of the day. And now she could barely keep her eyes open. Vard constantly cast her worried glances but said nothing, and she tried not to complain.

There had been little cover for them. One night Vard had found a cave, and another had been spent in a barn. The farmer and his wife had been kind but the hay loft was the best they would offer a pair of tatty travelers. Alecia couldn't blame them.

What farmer Baran and his wife told them was cause enough for them to be wary of strangers. The prince's men had made a call to the farm asking for more money when they had already paid their annual tithe. When Baran informed them he had none, the soldiers had conscripted Roser, the couple's adult son, into the Prince's Army. That had left Baran with only himself and his wife to work their holding. Small hope that Roser would be able to send money home on a soldier's wages.

Alecia's thoughts didn't improve her stomach. What was her father about? Was the extra money to be used to defend the kingdom or was it merely an excuse to line his pockets? Did he truly fear the raids by some unknown assailant that were troubling the outlying parts of the principality?

That was the other news Baran had whispered to Vard. There had been attacks on distant farms and small hamlets. Word hadn't come of who was responsible, but several farms and villages had been burned to the ground, the people having perished or fled to safety.

The news disturbed Alecia, and she could see Vard worried about the attacks as well. Perhaps it was not only her father's men they had to avoid?

Alecia felt a deep guilt at the plight of the Barans and all her people. She should be back in Brightcastle, championing their cause and fighting her father and his demands. Somehow she must find the means and the power to set things right in the kingdom. But she couldn't return under the threat of betrothal to Lord Finus. She felt shame at the thought but wouldn't sacrifice herself to Finus. There must be another way.

She roused from her dark thoughts as her horse waddled down the last shoulder of the mountains that separated Amitania from the northern reaches of the Kingdom of Thorius. The Usetar Mountain Range was barely tall enough to be called such, but the journey through the hills and valleys of the range had been treacherous nonetheless. The ground was rocky with large and small boulders strewn about, and smaller stones that rolled under the horses' feet. Alecia lifted her eyes to peer at the horizon, and could just make out a gray stone tower in the distance.

"That must be the lone tower of Amitania," she said, pointing. "It was the only tower left standing after the destruction of the city."

Vard had been scanning the forest between them and the ruined city, and he stared at the tower as if it could divulge its secrets. He had been more introverted each day they traveled closer to a possible mentor. Alecia hoped this sorcerer could help, for she didn't like the change in her captain.

"I don't like the feel of the forest between here and the ruins," he said.

Alecia laughed. It lightened her mood, if not that of her companion. "I have every faith in you, beloved."

He scowled. "Your faith is misplaced and your memory short. If you'll recall, it was you who rescued me after the last encounter with your father's hirelings."

That sobered her well enough. He was right. Even the strongest reached their limit on occasion. The Goddess knew she had almost reached hers before Vard rescued her. To think she had been ready to end her life! But she could well remember the despair at believing she had no alternative. Locked in her father's cellar, with only Lord Finus groping her to relieve the monotony, Alecia thought her life was over. That was when she believed her love for Vard wasn't returned. It was different now. She could face any challenge with him beside her.

Her arm cradled her abdomen and she could almost feel the life growing inside. Her monthly flows were still absent and the sickness grew daily. It could be nothing else. Her heart surged with joy at the thought of Vard's babe in her womb, but a stab of fear sliced through the elation and heightened her nausea. To be pregnant and on the road was a precarious thing. A fall from the horse could spell disaster, and what if she had to fight for her life or Vard's? Perhaps she should tell him? *No! He will dump me somewhere to brood and give birth.* She instinctively knew Vard would never risk the child and would be even more convinced he was a danger to her. She would have to mask the pregnancy for as long as possible. She could not abide to be separated from her love for longer than necessary. He would sideline her soon enough.

"It'll take the rest of this day and all tomorrow to cross that forest," Vard said. "Let's push on." He kicked his gelding into a walk and plunged beneath the trees.

They stopped for luncheon about an hour into the forest. Alecia had never seen trees so large or so close together. The light was too dim to see more than a few paces in front of her, but Vard had no trouble with his enhanced vision. His gold-flecked eyes magnified what light there was and they glowed when he looked at her. There was little sound besides the occasional rustle of a small creature under the leaves littering the forest floor. No groundcover grew beneath the trees except the moss that covered the many rocks and fallen trunks. The bole on which Alecia sat was damp from the mist that wove between the branches. When she looked up, the trunks penetrated a ceiling of fog, its tendrils drifting toward her. She shuddered at the thought those fingers of fog might solidify and pull her into the canopy.

"Are you cold, Alecia?" Vard asked.

"Just my imagination running wild." She rubbed her arms vigorously. "I don't like that fog. It seems to be reaching for me."

The haunting cry of a bird broke the silence and she jerked upright. "What was that?"

"Just a bird."

It sounded again but the cry became a screech, abruptly cut off.

"Now I know there's something out there." She stood and peered into the trees. "I've finished my meal, let's continue."

For a moment Vard didn't move but stood staring into the gloom. Alecia crossed to him and grasped his hand. There was a fine tension in his body as though he were ready to spring.

"Vard?"

He turned to her, his eyes fully golden.

"You're distracted," she said. "What is it?"

"My senses tell me to beware but I can't discern the threat. Let's mount and hasten through this patch of woods. It may improve as we ride."

Alecia did as he advised, not confident the forest would change for the better. She was right. The trees became denser and larger until she could reach out and touch a tree with either hand. The light dimmed and the blanketing fog formed a canopy that lay just out of reach. She felt she was being smothered beneath a damp blanket.

"Vard," she called softly, "I can't abide this much longer. It's oppressive."

"I'll look out for a place to camp," he called back. "A fire will cheer you."

As if *he* didn't need cheering! The prospect of spending a night in the soggy jungle made her wince. She swallowed several times to clear the lump in her throat but it wouldn't shift. Soon Vard indicated for her to stop, and he dismounted and entered the trees to the right of the track. He was gone only moments, but Alecia's fingers ached from clenching the reins by the time he returned.

"There's a small clearing and a rock overhang just through the trees." He helped her dismount. "Follow me." He seized Swift's reins and led the way.

Alecia's heart pounded. She swore Vard could hear it. He looked back at her and frowned, but at what she didn't know. The clearing was soon reached and indeed looked suitable. A large rock reared up out of the trees and curved a little to make a shallow roof. The remains of the last traveler's campfire lay to the front of the overhang.

Alecia raised her eyebrows when she saw the blackened logs. "At least we know someone has come this way. I was beginning to think we were the only ones left in the world."

Vard smiled. "There's dry wood at the back. I'll start a fire while you tie the horses."

Alecia reached for Swift's reins and suppressed a grunt as stabbing pain gripped her side. Vard didn't appear to notice. She loosened the saddles but left them on their mounts in case a quick getaway was needed. A repast of last night's roasted rabbit, very stale bread and crumbly goat's cheese was soon laid out on a blanket by the fire. Vard boiled water for tea. She ate hungrily. It felt like days since she had eaten, not hours, and her nausea had vanished with the light.

"We've only enough food for breakfast tomorrow," Vard said, "but perhaps Amitania may provide sustenance for us. Do you remember when you first told me about the lost city?"

Alecia's face grew hot. "It was our first outing," she said, "and our first kiss."

Vard grinned. "You accused me of believing in fairy tales. I liked the rumour that a powerful wizard had ensorcelled the people of Amitania, so they hoarded wealth and were overcome with hate for each other."

"I did not accuse!"

"And here we are, riding to find a sorcerer in that very same city." His eyes gleamed in the light from the fire.

Alecia's heart skipped a beat. He radiated danger, like a half-tame lion, or perhaps wolf was closer. Yes, Vard as a wolf could be described as half-tame. Vard as a bear, even with the amulet, was a different creature altogether.

She swallowed the twinge of nerves. "Do you think this might be the same sorcerer that the stories tell of? It's many centuries since Amitania thrived. He would be ancient."

"Anything is possible where sorcery is concerned, my love."

Alecia basked in the warm feeling she always had when he called her his love. A thought occurred. "How long do Defenders live?"

He frowned. "I don't know. My grandfather had the gift, but he died when I was very young. I remember nothing of him but a long white beard and piercing gold-flecked eyes."

"Just like yours," she murmured.

"My father didn't speak of the old man much, but he told me he died in a hunting accident. Where a Defender is concerned, that could mean anything."

"What animals could your grandfather become?"

"The hawk and the wolf. At least I never heard Father tell of the bear being a form that Poppa could take. I guess I'll never know for sure."

"And your father? He was an ordinary human?"

Vard nodded. "He and I were close until. . ."

Alecia clutched his hand and squeezed his fingers. He seemed glad of the contact.

He swallowed and went on. "The transformations began in my fourteenth summer. Father tried to help me as much as he could, but one day he vanished. His bow and quiver were gone, and a change of clothes. I never saw him again."

Alecia still gripped his fingers. "You were angry once when I told you that you would find him one day," she said. "I still believe that with all my heart."

"He is probably just a pile of bones in the bottom of some ravine, Alecia. For all I know, he just went hunting and fell upon trouble. When I was younger I used to tell myself we would meet again one day. I think it's something the young do to cope with loss. Once I passed my thirtieth year, I decided to let that particular fairy tale go." He looked at her. "You'll have to let yours go as well."

"What are you referring to?"

"Your father. Let the dream of a normal relationship with him go, Alecia. Be glad that you had a loving mother who gave you the strength to survive and the judgment to know right from wrong. You're blessed in that."

She laughed and didn't like the harsh sound of it. "You're the only blessing in my life, Vard. For the rest, the Goddess can take it and do with it what she will. I don't need my father. So you see, I've already let go of the dream of being close to him again."

"You haven't. But it's normal to delude yourself. I told myself I didn't care that I had lost everything dear to me, but when I realized I cared very much, I was able to grieve that loss. It will happen in its own time."

"Might we speak of something else?" She *had* let go of the dream of closeness with her father. Had she not been planning her revenge on him just that morning? "Let us remember something happy before we settle for the night." Alecia reclined in Vard's arms and they talked of their childhoods until they grew sleepy.

The next morning, Alecia awoke to a faint lightening of the forest that heralded the dawn. Vard was already up and had a fire crackling in the pit. After a breakfast of oatmeal, they retraced their steps to the trail and continued into the forest. The trees were as quiet as they had been the day before, except the mournful cry of an owl seemed to follow them as they rode. Alecia wished it would cease its serenade and go to sleep like owls should at that time of day. Even Vard appeared ill at ease. He rode with his hand on the hilt of his knife. Alecia imitated him, traveling just behind and to the right of Swift.

She tried to keep her mind on the surrounding trees, but the gentle sway of her horse lulled her mind. Before long, her eyes drooped. She began to sense movement in the trees to left and right but when she turned her head, there was nothing to be seen. She had just convinced herself that it was an illusion when a man swung out of the forest and landed in front of them on the trail. Their horses lurched to a halt, snorting and fussing.

Alecia's heart thudded and she blinked, trying to focus on the intruder whose skin was dark, almost black. He was tall and slender, clothed in a deep green tunic and leggings, knife at the hip and quiver over his shoulder. A short bow with a nocked arrow was trained on Vard. She experienced a moment's irritation that the man didn't think her worth his regard. She wished she could make out more of his features but the light was too poor.

Vard had frozen, and his eyes seemed locked on the man, his body poised for action.

The dark man slowly stood erect, his attitude all haughty self-assurance. His eyes had not left Vard. "Dismount and throw your weapons on the ground between us," he said, his voice deep and guttural, the words running together.

Vard dismounted and threw his knife and bow onto the road, then drew his sword and laid it gently atop the others. Alecia did the same and stepped back beside Vard.

"Who are you?" she asked and saw Vard shake his head out of the corner of her eye.

"You ride through *my* province and ask me that question?"

The man's eyes glowed in the gloom, and Alecia noticed that a dark headband with three silver leaves ringed his forehead. Short black curls covered his scalp leaving his small ears bare. If you could call them ears; they had no lobe and were pointed at the top.

"So this is your country?" Alecia asked.

"Mine and my brothers." At his words, a dozen dark men stepped onto the track. They had the grace of hunters and all carried small bows and long wicked knives. The headbands of the dozen had only two silver leaves. None looked friendly.

"Who are you?" the dark hunter asked.

"I am Anton," Vard said, "and this is my companion. . . Allandra. We seek passage through this forest to Amitania."

The leader made a gesture to the others and they surrounded Vard and Alecia, their knives extended. "Amitania has not existed for centuries."

Alecia bore the gaze of the dark man. Did his eyes have vertical pupils? "Regardless," she said, "that is where our journey takes us." She couldn't help the air of authority that infused her words. "I ask again, who are you?"

"I am Caele Aloe, the leader of this party of *Sis Lenweri*, and you are my prisoners. Do not try to escape."

"*Gir* Aloe, I didn't know your people inhabited these parts," Vard said.

Caele Aloe's eyebrows shot up. "You address me by my rank. You have experience of the *Lenweri*."

Vard nodded. "Your silver leaves denote a sergeant." He turned to Alecia. "*Gir* in their language. The *Lenweri* are elves. I've heard the *Sis Lenweri* are a faction of the *Lenweri*, intent on taking back kingdom lands."

"I don't intend to discuss *Sis Lenweri* goals with a human." Disgust hung thick on his words. "You will, however, get your wish, Anton," he said. "We will take you to Amitania, or what is left of it. My people have renamed it *Elvandang*. It is a place of dark magic such as the world has not seen. Our leader will decide what we should do with you and the woman, if woman she is. I have not seen a female of your kind dressed as a man before."

Alecia bristled. She stepped forward and met Aloe's eyes. No, they were not those of a cat, but the pupils were more oval than round. "I'm a woman, Aloe, and I'd appreciate it if you would call me… Allandra."

He seized her upper arm and she gasped as pain stabbed through her muscles. "Shut your mouth," he sneered. "There will be time enough for talking once you are presented at *Elvandang*." He turned to his men. "Bring the horses."

They formed up with Alecia and Vard in the center and the elves on all sides. Aloe set a brisk pace and soon Alecia was having difficulty keeping up. Her stomach cramps returned and she relied on her grip on Vard's arm to keep her moving forward.

Aloe called a halt. "At this rate we will never reach *Elvandang* before dark. What is the matter?"

Vard almost snarled. "Allandra is unwell. She can't keep up this pace. Let her ride."

"Watch what you demand. You have no power here, though it appears you are used to wielding it."

"Let her ride," Vard said.

The two men stood eye to eye as the seconds ticked past. Alecia would have held her breath if she had breath to spare but she was just grateful for the pause in the trek.

Finally, Caele Aloe grasped Alecia's arm and propelled her to her horse. She mounted and they continued on, setting a pace that meant her horse had to jog to keep up. The elves must be superhuman to have that stamina. The trotting of the horse was little better than being afoot. She was soon exhausted from the effort of controlling her movements in the saddle, so her side wouldn't cramp. She barely had time to notice the forest they rode through, though she saw Vard watching the trees as he always did.

Finally, blessedly, they slowed to a walk. The forest they passed through looked just the same. Was it a little lighter? The slower pace of the horse lulled Alecia in her exhausted state until she dozed. The next thing she experienced was being gently prized out of the saddle and cradled in strong arms. Her head lolled on a hard shoulder as she was taken into a dark place and laid on something soft that smelled of moss.

She roused herself and looked up as Vard moved away from the makeshift bed. "Where are we?" The walls around her were rough-hewn and moisture trickled down the stone. It smelled of earth and water and mold.

"Amitania, or what's left of it. We're beneath that stone tower we saw from the mountains. They have our weapons and refused to say how long we'd be kept here. How do you feel?"

She smiled. "I'm well, but this place is cold and… ugh." She shuddered and shook her hand as a cockroach scuttled across it. "I hate cockroaches."

"We're below ground in some type of chamber, perhaps these were dungeons."

"What are the *Lenweri* doing here?" she asked. "Father said he had sent them back to the farthest reaches of the north, that their numbers were so low they wouldn't trouble us for centuries."

Vard frowned. "I've been wondering the same thing. I've come across them before but further to the north when I was a lad. We'd occasionally trade with them. Back then, they were peace-loving."

"I don't think Father knows he has a hive of his old enemy this close to Brightcastle."

Vard joined her on the bed and pulled her against him. "They aren't on kingdom lands so perhaps not." He pulled her against his body. "Get some rest while you can and try not to worry."

Alecia snuggled against him and closed her eyes. Exhaustion made sleep come quickly.

CHAPTER 5

THE sound of grating metal woke Alecia. The wooden door swung into the room and Caele Aloe stood there, a burning brand in his hand. Shadows danced on the walls and a gust of wind threatened to extinguish the flame.

"You will come now. *Alen* Leth demands your presence. No doubt he would like to know why you dared to enter our realm." Aloe glared at them, his gaze unblinking.

She looked at Vard and he shrugged.

"Lead us to Lord Leth, *Gir* Aloe," Vard said.

Aloe led them out of the cell and another of the *Sis Lenweri* fell in behind them. Again a brisk pace was set, which Alecia found hard to match with her mind still fuzzy from sleep. They turned a corner and entered a long stone hall where they took a flight of steps to the surface. They exited through a trapdoor in the stone floor and she blinked in the weak light of a new day. At first, she thought she was in a forest, then began to make out the shapes of towers and pillars under the trees and vines. As she looked further she gasped at the size of the metropolis that stretched as far as the eye could see.

"My master does not like to be kept waiting," Aloe said, before leading off again through the jumbled stone.

Alecia had to pick her way with care but Vard was always close by to lend her an arm. As they walked through the ruins she saw few structures remained intact. In some areas, the elves came out to gaze at the strangers. They appeared to have used the loose rocks and stones to construct their own houses, weaving roofs out of vines. Smoke rose from chimneys in most of the residences. They picked their way along what must have been one of the main thoroughfares of the city, past the facades of once grand palaces and halls. The stone here was white and intricate carvings showed through the greenery. Alecia even saw the shimmer of quartz, much the same as the façade of her palace in Brightcastle. It was rumored that a witch had helped fashion the Zialni castle. Perhaps the same sorceress had helped construct the outer shell of these buildings.

Their journey brought them to a palace at the end of the promenade. They skirted the ruins of a gigantic dry fountain, which housed the statue of a woman, breast bared, one intact arm pointing at the palace as if showing the way. The head was missing, so Alecia could not have said whether the woman was accusing, directing or something else.

Broad steps led from the plaza to the front entry of the palace, the white stone cracked and broken in several places, though someone had tried to tidy as much as possible. Aloe led them straight up the steps and through the arched entry that had once held a door. Now there was nothing to bar their way, but Alecia felt a prickle up the hairs of her neck as they crossed the threshold. She looked at Vard and found him frowning. He stopped and Aloe spun to face him.

"What is it now, Anton?" His demeanor reeked of impatience and perhaps fear of keeping his master waiting.

"We just crossed a warding. Why is this place guarded by spells?"

"My master is a busy man. He likes to know who is close by, hence the magical barrier you call a warding." With that, he turned and strode off across the huge hall to another set of steps. These internal stairs had been restored, and they led to a circular gallery that gave access to numerous rooms. The doors to these rooms were decorated with flaking gold paint. Alecia stopped at the top of the stairs and looked around, but Aloe beckoned them on again to a door that lay just to the right at the top of the stairwell. He knocked and waited.

The door swung open, seemingly on its own, and a voice said, "Come." It had all the authority of absolute command.

Aloe stepped across the threshold, and Alecia followed along with Vard, wiping her suddenly clammy hands. She looked at Vard, but his eyes were riveted to the man who stood behind a desk in a corner of the room. He appeared not to be a kingdom man but neither was he elven. There was a nagging familiarity about him.

Alen Leth was large, as tall as Vard, with long graying hair and a neatly trimmed beard. He was dressed in a royal blue robe trimmed with gold thread, but the mantle couldn't hide his powerful shoulders and muscular torso. Alecia couldn't have said how old he was, but wrinkles marred his tanned visage. It was his eyes that captured her attention. The gold flecks in his irises were obvious even at that distance. She was trapped by his gaze, lost in its depth, mesmerized so she couldn't move.

"Come," Leth said, and Alecia moved forward, her eyes never straying from the man who commanded her, until an arm blocked her path.

"What are you doing?" Vard's voice shattered her trance. She broke the eye contact and gazed up at her beloved. He was addressing Leth.

"Never mind that," Leth said, "What are your names?" His stern tone left no room for defiance. It was a beautiful voice and Alecia imagined him serenading her. A ripple of anticipation ran up her spine at the thought.

Aloe stepped forward before Vard could speak. "The woman is Allandra and the man, Anton, or so they say. I suspect they are not their true names."

"It is no matter," Leth said. "The truth will out in good time." He turned to Alecia. "A woman in men's clothes. This is intriguing." He came out from behind the desk, and she watched as he slid his hand along the smooth wood. He possessed an artist's hands, with long fingers, and for some reason she imagined them on her body, giving her pleasure. Again his eyes trapped hers.

Leth walked around her and she fought the desire to grasp his hand. What was this? The only similar experience she could recall was when she first met Vard, but this was so much stronger. It was all she could do to resist this stranger with the compelling voice and hypnotic hands.

Leth paused in front of her. "You should be attired in silks and brocades not tunic and breeches. Though. . ." His eyes ran down and up her body, "this costume does show off your considerable attractions."

He looked at Aloe. "You will be handsomely rewarded for bringing this woman into my abode, *Gir* Aloe, well done."

"May I leave now, *Alen* Leth?" Aloe said.

Alecia glanced at the *Sis Lenweri* and found a troubled shadow in his gaze.

"Be about your duties, man." Leth's gaze shifted to Vard. "And Anton, in you I sense a kindred spirit, if a little underdeveloped." His eyes narrowed. "Do not be a fool, man. If you shift now, I will bind you in the transformation, so you will never leave your chosen form. Is that what you wish?"

A muscle twitched in Vard's jaw as he grasped the amber talisman at his throat. "I wish for your help." His voice was strained. "And I wish for you to keep your gaze from Allandra." Alecia watched the gold flecks in his stormy green eyes flare and subside with his control.

Leth snorted. "You're in my province, Anton. I hardly think you're in any position to make demands. What is this help you require?"

"I seek a shape shifter who can teach me my gift. Are you that man?"

"I think you know what I am but as to whether I am the one to teach you, only you can decide." A sly look came over his face. "You may stay and find out if you wish." He looked at Alecia. "Perhaps some exchange can be arranged."

"Allandra isn't part of the bargain," Vard snapped.

Leth's eyebrows climbed his forehead. "I do not need to bargain to attract a beautiful woman. It will be up to Allandra what she does. My bargain will be between you and me. Leave now and I will think on what you have said. *Ade* Gyndis will show you to your rooms where you can rest and break your fast. We will talk at a later time."

Leth turned his attention back to the papers on his desk, their presence seemingly forgotten. Alecia found herself disappointed to be leaving him.

They were guided from the room by the young *Sis Lenweri* corporal, back around the curving balustrade to rooms on the opposite side of the atrium. Gyndis ushered them into Alecia's room where a breakfast of steaming oats, fresh rolls and honey was laid out on an ancient stone table. Alecia immediately sat on a small stone bench, spooned honey and milk onto her porridge and reveled in the first fresh meal she had had in a week. She didn't feel ill this morning but was ravenously hungry. Her eyes followed Vard as he inspected the room, flicking a tapestry aside and peering from the windows and into a tall wooden cupboard.

"What is the matter, dearest?" she asked, between mouthfuls of oats. "Come and break your fast. You must be starving."

"This place unnerves me. Something isn't right." He paced across the room and turned to face her. "First we are treated like criminals and now we are guests." His eyes fell to the feast before him. "But I *am* hungry."

"Then put aside your worries and eat. We must be grateful for small fortunes."

Vard broke a bread roll, spooned honey onto it and used the bread to scoop the porridge into his mouth. "This could be a trap of your father's making."

Alecia laughed. "Your old soldier's habits amuse me, Vard," she said, eyes sparkling as she watched him shovel his breakfast in, as he had on the road. "Lord Leth has provided utensils for us. We have not been on the road so long that our manners should desert us. As for the other, I don't think my father's arm stretches this far. As you said earlier, we're not in the kingdom now."

"I wouldn't like to get a nasty surprise." His sharp green eyes snapped to hers. "Leth leers at you. He isn't all that commanding, but you seemed mesmerized by him."

"I did feel trapped by his gaze." Alecia poured a cup of strong tea laced with honey. "You'll have to ensure that he doesn't entrance me completely. I found myself imagining strange things as he talked. He'd be a hard man to say 'no' to."

Vard frowned at her. "Then make sure you are never alone with him. Perhaps it's part of the Defender persona."

Alecia smiled at him. He was so naïve at times. "*You* have a little of it, you know. You don't use it as Leth does but I see the effect you have on women. I've felt it. You're difficult to ignore, and it's not just your devastating good looks that draw the eye."

He blushed for the first time Alecia could remember. She laughed gaily as she leaned across the table to pat the hard stubble on his jaw. "That's what I love about you, Vard. Just when I think I know you, you surprise me. I never thought you capable of embarrassment."

He stood and walked away from the table, a sudden frown erasing the blush of moments before. She hurried to his side.

"I'm sorry, beloved," she said. Her eyes roved hungrily over his body, from the hard planes of his face and gorgeous sea-green eyes to his broad shoulders and lean hips. He was all she wanted and more, and he was the father of her unborn child, for she was certain now that Vard's babe grew within her. She pressed her body to his and gazed up at him. His arms enclosed her and she marveled again at how their bodies complemented each other. His arousal pushed against her.

"No need for apologies, Alecia," he said, his eyes becoming golden with excitement before the pupils obliterated the gold. His lips met hers and she felt a week of pent-up passion driving his mouth and hands. She responded, her hands curling up into his hair and working their way down his chest to the fastening of his breeches.

Vard pulled back. "Are you sure, my love?"

Alecia's heart cried at the doubt in his voice. "I want you more than anything. You're all I've ever wanted since that day in the meadow when we kissed for the first time."

"But you've been so distant this past week, I wondered if you regretted leaving your father." She knew by his look that he still wondered.

"I regret nothing, beloved. I know I've been withdrawn but you mustn't think you're the cause. I've been tired and feeling unwell. That's all." She pushed herself against him and kissed him long and passionately before leading him toward the bed. "Make love to me, Vard. I've missed you."

He scooped her into his arms, laid her gently on the furs that covered the bed and joined her. She gasped as his hand came to rest on her abdomen. Something had moved in her belly. The child? Did it feel its father's hand?

The desire in Vard's eyes was instantly replaced by concern. "What is it? Do you feel pain?"

Alecia pushed her nagging fear of the unknown aside and drew his head closer. "It's nothing. Now kiss me." She brought his lips to hers and rolled on top of him, surprised at the passion that overcame her. In seconds, Vard's clothes were stripped away and hers followed. Their coupling was almost spiritual, as if they strived to become one. Alecia could not get close enough to the man she loved, even when he rested within her. Again she felt the babe move in her womb as if it too jumped with joy at the presence of its father.

Afterward, they lay naked under the furs, Vard's leg across her hips, his fingers playing with a strand of her long blonde hair. She had never seen such love in his eyes and knew the experience had stirred his soul as it had hers.

"Never leave me," she said, her heart skipping a beat at the mere thought of a life without him. "I couldn't live if you should leave me. Promise."

The love of a moment before was replaced with fear, the brilliant green of his eyes became a stormy sea. "I promise I'll always protect you, Alecia. That's the best I can do. I couldn't live if I caused your death."

She sat up in bed, the furs slipping until they barely covered her breasts. For once, she didn't care. She was with child to this man and they shared a bond even greater than that. Her heart was tied to him beyond death. Couldn't he feel that? She clutched his hand and placed it over her heart. They both gasped at the spark that the touch of their skins always evoked.

"My heart beats for you, because of you, with yours," she said, her gaze boring into his. "If you leave me I'll die. My body may live on for a while, but I'll be dead in spirit, and what does life mean when the spirit is dead?"

Vard drew his hand away but his eyes never left hers. "You have a flair for the dramatic that all women seem to share. It's not easy to be responsible for the death of another, especially when they are beloved."

"Don't you think I know that? Don't you think it was difficult for me to accept what I've done in the past? I still have nightmares about the deaths of those mercenaries."

"Think how much worse it would be if you loved those men. If one had been your best friend, your brother? Ask as often as you like, Alecia, but I won't be responsible for your death. I pray the Goddess will give me the strength to walk away if I must."

Tears filled her eyes. "I was dead," she said, her voice breaking. "I was dead in that dungeon until you rescued me. Your love revived my spirit. How can your memory be that poor? You once made me promise I would not take my own life. I held to that promise. It was all that sustained me in the days I was held prisoner by my father, when Finus's hands pawed me. But now we are one, the only promise that will sustain me is yours."

Vard slid from the bed, covering himself with a sheet. His eyes found hers again. "I won't promise to let you die. All I can hope is that you'll be safe until I know if Leth is the teacher I seek. The Goddess knows I should send you away now but I'm too weak. You know the amulet isn't the answer we once thought. Who can tell how long the enchantment will last this time? If I fail to learn enough control from Leth to keep you safe, I must distance myself. Accept that Alecia. I don't wish to quarrel with you. My heart is yours but I won't live knowing I caused your death."

She climbed from the bed, not trying to shield her body from Vard's hot gaze. She dressed and left the room without another word.

Chapter 6

V ARD'S skin tingled with the sixth sense that had warned him of danger on more than one occasion. Where was Alecia? If not for his distress when she left the room he would've followed her immediately, instead of standing transfixed for long moments after the door closed behind her. He stood on the balcony that ran in a circle around the building, but she was not to be seen. He couldn't just barge into rooms indiscriminately, hoping to find her.

He turned left and walked toward Leth's quarters, pausing outside to place his ear at the door.

"Can I help you?" a voice said at his elbow.

Vard spun, stifling the curse that sprang to his lips, and encountered *Ade* Gyndis who had shown them to their rooms. The corporal's eyes narrowed at something he saw in Vard's face.

"I was seeking Al. . . Allandra, the woman who travels with me."

"Ah, yes. She has caught the eye of our leader and I can see why. Our women are darker and more slender but there is a fire within her that puts me in mind of our *Lenweri* females."

Vard frowned and drew himself up. "Do you know where she is?"

"I saw her walking with *Alen* Leth in the grove behind the palace. If you descend to the level below and exit via the passage that lies beneath your rooms, it will take you directly there. But I warn you. *Alen* Leth does not like to be disturbed, especially when he is entertaining."

"I'll bear that in mind," Vard growled and left without thanking the soldier. He circled the balcony and descended the staircase, all the while clutching the amber talisman. If that man had harmed Alecia…

He strode along the passage and through open wrought iron gates into a paradise. Gigantic trees lined the path, and Vard spied the verdant grass of a sunny clearing at the other end. But that couldn't be possible when the sky was thick with clouds that threatened snow. The hair on the back of his neck stirred.

The path was only twenty paces long but it was twilight under the trees. He inched his way, his steps silent on the dirt and leaves underfoot. His gut told him to beware. At the end of the pathway, he peered around the bole of a huge oak and spied Leth and Alecia seated on a bench in front of a fountain. Water splashed from the mouth of a stone bear that reared above them. Vard swallowed fear as he saw Alecia's hands held fast in Leth's.

"There you are, Allandra," he said as he stepped onto the grass of the clearing. Neither Alecia nor Leth moved and Vard fought down another surge of dread. "What's going on?" His voice, forced past the tightness in his throat, was a harsh croak.

Vard didn't think he imagined the flash of fury that crossed Leth's bronzed features.

"Allandra and I were only chatting, weren't we?" he said, looking at Alecia. He stood and faced Vard, the long blue sleeves of his robe sweeping outward. Vard tensed, expecting an attack, but Leth laughed, his rich tones striking a discordant note.

The break in contact seemed to release Alecia and she turned on her seat. "Isn't this a marvelous place?" she said, the dreamy note of her voice warning Vard she had been under the lord's spell. "Who would have thought that there could be sunshine in this place? Lord Leth said it has broken through just for me."

"Come to me, Allandra." Vard held out his hand, keeping an eye on Leth's imposing figure. A frown rippled across Alecia's face but she stood and moved to Vard's side. "I want you to make your apologies to Lord Leth and wait for me in your room," he said, trying to place the power of the Defender into his look and words. He had no idea if he succeeded in this, but Alecia frowned up at him again and then turned back to Lord Leth.

"I feel tired, My Lord," she said. "Would you excuse me?"

He frowned but nodded, and she turned and left without another word.

"There is a story behind that one, and you for that matter," Leth said, staring after Alecia. "She shows no inclination to curtsy to me, even though she should see me as her superior. That tells me much."

"Forget Allandra," Vard snapped, striding past and stopping at the stone bench so Leth had to turn to face him. "I wish to know if you will teach me my heritage."

"Blunt, aren't you?"

"I'm in great need and lives are at risk."

"I can see that is true, but a bargain must be struck. There must be some reward in this for me." He stared into Vard's eyes.

Vard felt himself grow cold. "I told you Allandra isn't part of any bargain." He clutched his amber talisman between shaking fingers.

"Your control is tenuous," Leth said. "When it snaps, what happens to your precious woman then?" He watched Vard closely and smiled. "I see it has already happened. What of next time. Will she survive? Give her to me and you will not need to worry."

"Allandra isn't my property to be passed around," Vard ground out through clenched teeth.

"Even so, your attachment to her must give you sleepless nights. Why lie awake imagining that soft white flesh torn, those beautiful eyes unseeing, when you can save her from that?"

"That's precisely what I'm trying to do."

"Without losing her. You're in love with her," Leth spat, contempt thick in his voice. "She will be your undoing. Give her to me."

"I've already said no," Vard insisted, his voice low, his control balanced on a knife edge. It was as though Leth wished to push him over that edge.

Leth took a deep breath and broke eye contact. Vard allowed his tensed muscles to relax one by one.

"Very well," Leth said. "We shall see about the woman, Allandra. I will make another bargain for now. My people require training. The *Lenweri* are forest people, skilled in the use of the short bow and the knife, but they lack prowess with the sword and the longbow. I wonder if you could teach them the necessary skills."

"Why?"

"You don't need to know that, Anton, if that is your name."

"It *is* my name."

"Perhaps."

"There's little trust between us," Vard said, forcing the words between gritted teeth. "What will you teach me, when, and for how long?"

"How long will it take to train two thousand of my *Lenweri*?"

Vard's heart stuttered at the thought of that many elven warriors. "I'd have to know their skill level to tell you that."

"But you have the necessary expertise for the job?"

"I do. What will you teach me?"

"When I have finished with you, you will know all there is to know about your gift."

Vard nodded. "Show me your soldiers."

Vard strode alongside Leth as the mysterious lord made his way back, through the trees and the palace passage, and out into the ruined square. Rain fell in a cold drizzle that had not been present in the garden.

Vard stared at Leth, his palms upraised to catch the raindrops. "Is this the style of gift that you'll impart, Leth? The ability to order the weather?"

"I'm afraid not," the older man said. "I have many talents, not all of them Defender in origin. Now we must hurry if we are to see the troops before they disperse for maneuvers."

Leth strode off across the square, heading toward a large arch. Vard followed, and they entered a wide street where fallen stone blocks, too large for a man to move alone, lay against the walls. The houses and palaces on either side had partially crumbled and the resulting rubble had yet to be properly cleared. Vard's boots sent shards of stone skittering across the paving stones. He couldn't comprehend why the streets hadn't been cleared, unless it was to hinder the movement of enemies. The gaping holes in the walls above made Vard uneasy. The street was silent except for their footfalls. There were no doors leading off the street into the buildings, and plenty of high vantage points for archers. If an enemy were to enter, few would escape an attack here.

The wide street eventually led into a huge space that appeared to be a staging ground, with numerous doors in the walls on the four sides that bordered it. The square was a bustle of activity, with horses being shod inside a building to the right, while elves trained in various activities throughout the open space. The tall, lithe *Lenweri* were paired up and taking part in hand to hand combat. A small group were practicing archery in a corner partitioned off by bales of straw, while another group watched two elves fighting with practice swords.

Leth stood with his powerful arms folded across his chest, a frown on his face. "I am told that the short bows are fine for horseback or in confined spaces but longbows would be an advantage in battles on a larger scale. Do you agree?"

Vard frowned. Was the man trying to catch him out? "Generally, that's true. Long bows enable you to engage with the enemy before they can engage with you. What do you have planned?"

"That is information you do not need to know."

"There may come a time when I'll require that information or else make costly blunders."

"I will await that time."

Vard turned back to watch the fighters.

"Do you think you can improve their combat skills?" Leth asked.

"Undoubtedly. When do I begin?"

"Now. Spend the rest of this day with the troops and dine with me tonight. I will begin your tuition after dinner. Until then." Leth spun on his heel and stalked off in the direction of the palace.

Vard turned back to the staging ground and ran an eye over his charges. How was he supposed to convince them he was there to instruct them? The agreement had just been reached. Leth had no opportunity to inform any of the men they had a new trainer. He knew how he'd react if he were in their place. Vard spotted a familiar face outside the smithy. Caele Aloe leaned against the stone wall, his hostile gaze fixed on Vard. No help from that quarter then.

His sword and longbow were still held by Leth and his cronies, but Vard could demonstrate sword skills with the practice lathes the *Sis Lenweri* were using. Eyes fixed on the soldier supervising, Vard walked across the staging ground, ignoring the glances from the elves he passed. They were far from friendly but no one stopped him. Aloe still glared at him from the blacksmith's.

Vard pushed through the ring of spectators and stopped a few paces from the swordsmen, just as a large *Sis Lenweri* with a shaven scalp and half his left ear missing struck his opponent on the side of the head. He went down and stayed down. Vard flinched. A knock by a practice sword on the head could be fatal. The bald fighter played for keeps. He spied Vard and turned to face him.

"Step up, kingdom man, and I will show you how the *Sis Lenweri* fight."

"Just a moment, Arthoe," the trainer said, placing his hand on the bald man's chest. He looked at Vard. "I am *Gir* Ensalor, the sword master. Explain your presence here."

Vard met the trainer's steady gaze. "Lord Leth has enlisted my help to train this bunch of forest dwellers. I must say he's right to be concerned, from what I see."

"Is he?" Ensalor's voice sounded ominous. "Why should *Alen* Leth be so concerned, kingdom man?"

Vard allowed his gaze to sweep around the watching faces. "One charge from kingdom soldiers and this sorry excuse for a fighting force would crumple. I suspect they are much more used to sneaking up on their enemies and killing them in their sleep."

Angry muttering surged around the assembled *Sis Lenweri*.

Ensalor, burly for an elf, held up his hand and the men fell silent. Vard nodded approvingly. At least they were disciplined.

"What is your name?" Ensalor asked.

"Anton."

"Would you care to show us where we are weak, Anton?" The trainer stepped away and Arthoe leaped toward Vard, practice sword raised, a roar of fury blasting from him.

Vard spun out of the way of a vicious strike aimed at his throat and scooped up the practice sword of the fighter Arthoe had downed. He turned to confront the elf, but Arthoe was already on his way back, sword raised, sweat glistening on his dark skin. Fury blazed from his eyes and Vard's heart soared. The elf was too angry. Vard blocked a savage thrust and swept Arthoe's blade aside, using his momentum to carry him past the fighter. With lighting speed, Vard spun and brought his blade down in a resounding crack across the fighter's back. Arthoe went down, his bare skin split by the force of the wooden sword.

Silence greeted Vard's victory and he stepped backward out of Arthoe's reach. Had the scarred fighter been their champion? No matter. They'd learn hero worship had no place in the fighting ranks. He was here to forge new skills, but what were those new skills to be directed against? Were his suspicions correct? Was Leth forming a fighting force that would come against the King's army?

He raised his voice to the watching men, many of whom scowled at him. No, they didn't like what he had done to Arthoe. "Strength and aggression are important characteristics in a warrior," he said, walking around the circle. "But these traits must be tempered with patience and finesse. You must feel at one with the sword to engage in the dance. You require perfect balance, and you must never allow your heart to rule your mind." He paused to allow his words to have their full effect. "Those who wish to master their mind and learn the dance of the swordfighter may meet with me here tomorrow at dawn." He looked down at Arthoe. "Any who think they know better need not attend."

As Vard turned to leave, a growl sounded from Arthoe's direction. Vard kept walking. It seemed he really would have to make an example of the elven champion. When he gauged Arthoe was about to strike he spun to the left, swinging the practice sword he still held against his assailant's temple. Arthoe went down in a heap and the men nearest crowded around the body, fingering his throat.

"He lives. Get the healer," someone said, but Vard dropped the practice sword and walked away. As he cast his eye around the staging ground, he saw he had drawn the gaze of many other *Sis Lenweri* as well.

"Nothing like making a good first impression," he muttered. The hostile stares made his skin itch and the hairs stand on his neck. Time to find Alecia.

CHAPTER 7

VARD frowned at himself in the cracked mirror above the washstand in his room. He looked ridiculous. The robes supplied by Leth fit him well, but robes weren't his style. The fabric was black silk with golden embroidery around the collar and sleeves, and the swishing sound he made when he moved anywhere was altogether too feminine. How did men ever become used to wearing these. . . dresses?

"Ah, *Anton*, how wonderfully mystical you look this evening," Alecia said from behind him.

How had he not heard her enter? *Damned clothes!*

"Don't mock me, *Allandra*, or I'll put you across my knee and spank your adorable behind." His gaze met hers in the mirror.

Alecia's eyes widened until their lilac seemed to encompass her entire face. "You wouldn't dare!"

Vard turned, prepared to take Alecia in his arms but his mouth went dry with one glance at her. "Where did you get that?"

She frowned and flipped the sleeve of his robe. "It's not only you who'll look splendid this evening." She twirled in front of him, tossing back her head and laughing as he hadn't heard her laugh since... Vard couldn't remember when he'd last heard Alecia sound truly happy. That was enough to sour his mood even further. He should never have allowed her to leave Brightcastle.

He reached out and clasped her arms, forcing her to stand still as he scrutinized her dress. It was crimson silk with fine silver embroidery across the bodice and tiny silver buttons that ran up her spine. The bodice was fitted to the hips, ably demonstrating Alecia's full bosom, and the skirt fell to a small train at the back. Her hair was piled on her head with loops of scarlet ribbon and a silver and ruby tiara completed the ensemble.

"Isn't this the most delightful costume you've ever seen?" she said, her hands caressing the soft folds of fabric at her hips.

"You can't go before Leth dressed like that."

She scowled at him. "Why ever not? Oh, Vard, I'd forgotten how it felt to dress like this. I mean, I'd give up anything for you, and I have, but… I never realized how much I enjoyed looking pretty."

He chuckled wryly. "You look so much more than 'pretty'. But that isn't what I meant. If Leth sees you in that dress, he'll know you for the princess you are. The way you carry yourself in that gown, you couldn't be anything else. He'll see that right away. And that tiara. . . Is it possible he already knows? Why else would he give that to you?"

Alecia frowned and chewed her lip. "I hadn't thought of that. I was too excited at wearing this magnificent gown after over a month in dirty breeches and tunics." She watched Vard closely as she spoke. "But don't feel guilty, beloved. It's not your fault that my father tried to use me." She wound her arms around Vard's waist. "I'd give up gowns for you any day. How could you think I'd put up with a lecherous husband just to wear the clothes of a princess? I'm not that shallow."

"I know you're not shallow, Alecia, but my heart breaks to see you reduced as you are."

"Let's not talk of these things, lest we be overheard. Leth may not know anything of who I am." An impish smile flashed onto her face. "I'll pretend not to know what I'm doing at dinner and he'll be none the wiser."

Vard grinned back. "I look forward to that." He pulled her close and closed his eyes as their lips met, reveling in the feel of her soft curves against his hardness. She was intoxicating, her hold on him so powerful he wondered at times if he *could* walk away, even to save her life. He prayed he'd never have to find out. If Leth could teach him his gift, he might never have to leave Alecia.

He pulled his lips from hers and smiled. "It's time for dinner, beloved."

Alecia blinked as if coming out of a trance. "I think your Defender skills might be coming to the fore, Vard," she whispered. "I feel as if I've been ensorcelled. Are you sure you're not practicing on me?"

"It's the sorcery of love, nothing more." He offered his arm and she drew close. The heat of her body stirred his blood, made him wish they could enjoy an intimate dinner in her room, rather than with their host.

* * *

Leth awaited them in a small dining room adjoining his office. He sat at the head of a candlelit table sipping from a silver goblet. A beautiful *Lenweri* woman stood at his elbow, clothed in a scandalously sheer dress of close-fitting black silk. Alecia was glad the light was too low to reveal more of her form. She glanced at Vard and found him studying the elven woman, a frown on his face.

Alecia turned her attention to Leth and wished immediately she hadn't. His penetrating golden gaze seemed to take in every detail of her appearance as though he wanted to brand it into his memory. She swallowed and attempted a smile, but his eyes met hers at that moment. Her heart flipped. She couldn't move, nor look away.

"Allandra," Leth said, his deep voice sending shivers over her skin, "you are exquisite. That color suits you and the style is perfect. You look like a princess."

Leth left the words hanging as if to invite discussion, but Vard stepped in front of her and the lord's spell over Alecia was broken.

"Thank you for the garments, *Alen* Leth," Vard said.

He sounded on edge, but Alecia only half listened to his words. She was occupied examining Leth while his attention was elsewhere. The imposing lord wore robes similar to Vard's but of crimson silk with silver embroidery, matching her gown perfectly. His long fingers caressed the silver goblet and she had to force her eyes away again. She raised her gaze, expecting to see a silver crown studded with rubies, but was relieved to find Leth's grey-streaked dark hair bare of adornment.

She crossed to the table to sit as far from her host as possible, but the *Lenweri* woman moved toward her and pulled out a chair closer to Leth.

"Please sit here, Mistress," the woman said, her musical voice pleasing.

Alecia couldn't stop a frown as she stood and moved two chairs closer to Leth. At least she would be facing Vard. That might help keep her thoughts where they needed to be.

Leth and Vard seemed to be involved in a staring match that gave Alecia more time to study her host. He was difficult to put an age to, but the wrinkles and graying hair told her he was a good deal older than Vard, perhaps fifty summers. His presence drew the eye and his voice demanded to be listened to.

"Sit, Anton," he said, pointing to the place opposite Alecia. "We are ready, Failora," he said to the elven woman. Her fingers brushed Leth's sleeve as she walked past him and left the room.

Alecia was paralyzed by Leth's gaze once again. "I knew you were created to wear gowns, Allandra. Do they not feel wonderful against your skin after being on the road for. . . how long did you say?"

"We didn't say, *Alen* Leth," Vard said into the pause.

Didn't he trust her to give the right answer?

"It's not important how long we have traveled," Vard said. "You and I have struck a deal. I'll train your soldiers and you'll train me. You've been reticent at presenting me with information as to the reason for the training. Trust must be earned. I think you know enough of us for now."

Leth stood abruptly, his face red and eyes blazing. Alecia stifled a squeak of fear. *What's wrong with me? Why should I act like a frightened mouse?*

Vard surged to his feet and the men stood glaring at each other.

"I am the Master," Leth said. "You are here at my sufferance after blundering into my kingdom. It was you who sought my help. How dare you insult me?" His hands shook as they gripped the table. Alecia thought she heard the wood groan.

Please say something, Vard.

Vard flicked her a look and turned back to Leth. "I'm sorry to have upset you. Trust doesn't come easily for me."

"Hold your tongue in future or face the consequences," Leth roared, slamming his fist down on the table and spilling red wine over the snowy cloth. "Failora!"

Failora hurried in through one of the two doors in the back wall, her movements graceful even in haste. She moved the plates and utensils to the side and Leth passed his right hand over the stain and muttered words under his breath. The wine stain faded as Alecia looked on and Failora re-laid the setting. She left and returned with their meals. Leth resumed his seat.

"You would do well to remember who is master here." Leth glared at Vard, his anger under control but not extinguished. "Let us forget unpleasantness and enjoy the food that Failora has prepared. Thanks and praise be to Avorelph."

"Praise to Avorelph," Alecia murmured, looking across at Vard. The gold flecks in his green eyes were conspicuous. *Please Goddess, let him keep his temper.* They couldn't afford for him to enter the transformation. Anything might happen if Leth felt threatened, and Alecia suspected Vard's talents would appear child-like beside their host's.

"Who is Avorelph, Lord Leth?" Alecia asked, lifting her fork to spear a plump battered ball of something or other.

Leth seemed to be still composing himself and took a moment to answer. "Avorelph is a previous *Lenweri* king who became a god of the people. He is *the* most important elven god in my opinion. He was a celebrated warrior, and the *Lenweri* see in him a great hope for their future." Leth's voice echoed around the chamber, even though he spoke quietly. Did he use sorcery to make his voice travel?

Alecia could see that conversation along these lines was not wise. "What do we eat?" She placed the golden crispy ball into her mouth and it popped, releasing a delicious, salty liquid when she bit down on it.

"Ah, my dear, I am glad you asked. The balls are mountain goat's eyeballs, and the meat is goat meat shredded and rolled in goat's stomach then baked in a wrapping of ivy leaves."

Alecia gagged and breathed deeply through her nose, the remnants of the eyeball sloshing on her tongue. She couldn't spit it out here! She'd have to swallow it. Alecia struggled to compose her face as the eyeball slid down her throat. Eyes closed, she battled rising bile and shuddered. When she opened her eyes, Leth was smiling. Her face flamed and he laughed out loud.

"You are delightful, Allandra. Your manners are impeccable even though the thought of the goat's eyeball clearly repulsed you. You intrigue me!"

Alecia frowned at her lap and snuck a quick glance at Vard. His face was like thunder. Too late, she remembered she was supposed to be acting as though she had no court manners. She turned to the side and spat onto the floor, observing Leth from the corner of her eye. She thought his eyebrows climbed his forehead but if she looked his way now it would spoil the effect. Vard's expression was bland as he returned to his meal. She watched him eat his food as though he relished the fare. Weren't ivy leaves poisonous? She pushed her plate away, seized her goblet and swallowed the wine inside with an audible gulp. Failora glided over to refill the vessel and Alecia took another large swig which she choked on.

Droplets of red wine sprayed from her mouth all over the snowy tablecloth and onto Vard's plate, but Alecia was more concerned with drawing fresh air into a throat closed by the sweet liquid. As she drew in wheezing breaths and fought for more air, Vard shoved his chair back and appeared at her side. He hauled her from her chair and drew her arms above her head, murmuring soothingly. Slowly her panic calmed and the black spots left her vision. She drew a shuddering breath and settled back onto her chair.

Vard gave her a last pat on the shoulder and resumed his seat, while Failora hustled over with a moist warm cloth to wipe her face.

"Thank you," Alecia said as she took the cloth from the woman. The damp fabric felt good on her skin and she buried her face in its folds until her breathing returned to normal.

"A most interesting dinner guest you are, Allandra," Leth said, his dark eyes amused. "I believe Failora has prepared a broth. Would you like her to remove your meal and fetch you the soup?"

"Thank you, *Alen* Leth," Alecia said, her voice still raspy after her coughing fit. "You are kind to consider me that way. I'm sorry I disturbed your meal."

"It is nothing, Allandra. A man must endure all manner of upset if he is to have the company of a beautiful woman. Ah, here is the broth now. Enjoy."

The soup was delicious, and Alecia tried to appear as clumsy as possible. Quite a lot fell on the tablecloth and she even managed to dip her sleeve in her meal. All in all, it wasn't a bad approximation of a woman with few table manners, she thought.

The main course over, Failora brought a rich goat's cheese with crusty bread and a tub of mountain lemon citrus marmalade, which was delicious with the cheese. Vard disdained the preserve but Leth smeared it on his bread before topping it with thick slabs of the cheese.

"I see you appreciate the combination, Allandra. I have found nothing like it and I have traveled far. It shows an adventurous palate, one that has been exposed to a range of foods." He laughed suddenly and Alecia jumped. "All except mountain goat's eyeballs, that is."

Alecia blushed again. She wasn't doing a good job of appearing uncultured, but perhaps she had confused Leth with her clumsiness. She would be more careful in future and decline his dinner invitations. Vard could dine with the lord without her. She frowned. That might not be such a good idea. He could easily lose his temper with a few well aimed jibes from Lord Leth.

"Bring the tea if you please, Failora," Leth said, pushing his chair back and rising from the table. "I say tea," he said, "but it's liberally laced with fortified wine. Just the thing to round off a meal." He looked at Alecia. "Perhaps you would like to pass on the tea, Allandra?"

She inclined her head. "Perhaps I will do so, Lord Leth. If you'll excuse me, I'll retire to my room. I'm weary after the ordeal of the past days."

Leth came forward and raised her hand to his mouth. She watched, mesmerized as his lips brushed her fingers. The power of the gesture overwhelmed her. She raised her eyes to his and felt the full force of Leth's gaze. The gold flecks enlarged, merged then seemed to blaze out, searing into her and leaving her skin tingling. His lips curved in a knowing smile.

"Until we meet again," he said, releasing her fingers and turning away.

Vard's arm curved around her waist as he turned her gently to face him. "Sleep soundly, beloved. I'll look in on you after our lesson."

He led her to the door and watched as she walked to her chamber. She waved to him from her door and slipped inside.

The room was warm from the fire that blazed in the hearth. She stripped her gown and stood in front of a long mirror that had once boasted a gilded frame. Now only specs of gold showed along the weathered wood, as if the piece had lain outdoor. She turned to the side and ran her hands over her abdomen. Was it swelling? No, it was too early yet, but what would she do when she was too large to fit into her breeches? She couldn't tell Vard too soon for fear he'd send her away. Perhaps she shouldn't worry. After all, *Alen* Leth would teach Vard all the tricks of the Defender and she would no longer be at risk of his self-control. Then they could live happy and safe forever as husband and wife.

Alecia thought of the people of Brightcastle whom she had abandoned. She couldn't leave them at the mercy of Prince Zialni and Lord Finus. She must find a way to remove her father and his hated advisor without placing her child in danger. Somehow, she'd take her rightful place as the ruler of Brightcastle, and perhaps one day, queen of the kingdom, just as her idol Izebel had done. But there was much to accomplish before her dreams would be realized. Leth was the first hurdle she and Vard must overcome.

A shudder rippled up her spine and Leth's face floated into her memory. Was he the dark sorcerer she had dreamt of? There were similarities. If they were one and the same, Vard must be careful. Her dreams carried the threat of treachery. She could remember nothing specific, but instinctively knew the man in her dreams couldn't be trusted.

She spied her breeches and tunic on the floor near the fire and donned them. If Leth planned treachery, in what form would it come? Alecia drifted around the room, mulling over the dark dreams and the feelings she had concerning Leth. She must discover more about the enigmatic lord. What better time than right now, when he was occupied with Vard? She grabbed her cloak and slipped from the room.

Chapter 8

VARD turned from the door to find Leth studying him. "I hope you can confide in me, Anton," the sorcerer said, his deep voice reverberating around the stone walls. "We cannot have a healthy relationship as teacher and student if you harbor secrets."

Vard crossed the room and sat in one of two overstuffed armchairs near the hearth, leaving Leth standing beside the mantle. He fixed the lord with a challenging stare, which was returned in full measure. How dare he lecture *Vard* about secrets! He had not been at all forthcoming about his intentions regarding the training of the *Sis Lenweri*.

Leth frowned. "I admire your courage. Not many men could stare me down and live. It is fortunate you are somewhat more of an equal than most. I will grant you a measure of leniency when it comes to your behavior around me, but know that I expect you to show proper deference when we are in public. I'll not have the men witness your insubordination."

"Is that a condition of your tutoring?"

"You may see it as such," the lord said. "Now let us begin. We will practice bringing ourselves to the brink of transformation and holding it steady. Do not transform."

Vard walked back around the upper balcony to Alecia's room. His emotions jumped from fury to despair and back again, mixed with a healthy measure of frustration. The lesson had been a waste. His muscles ached with fatigue. Bruises covered his shoulders and torso from the restraint Leth had used when the transformations took hold. The sorcerer could wrap Vard up with magical bonds, like a babe in swaddling, whenever he wished, and he had done so frequently over the past two hours.

No matter how hard he tried, Vard couldn't hold himself on the brink of transformation without using the stone. Leth didn't use any such focus and had forbidden Vard to use his amber talisman during the lessons. Leth's changes from man to hawk to wolf to snake occurred smoothly. Vard despaired of ever achieving such control of his gift, and if he couldn't control it he'd lose Alecia, one way or another.

The bitter thought consumed him as he entered her room and crossed to the fireplace. He removed a burning stick and lit the candle on the bedside table. His gut went cold. Alecia wasn't in bed.

He lit another candle and checked in the wardrobe and under the bed. Alecia wasn't in her room. Where would she go? Had she left of her own free will? He pushed worry aside and took a deep breath. Her gown lay discarded on the floor. He picked it up but saw no signs of violence. There were no blood stains on the floor, but her tunic and breeches were missing along with her soft boots.

She must have changed and left her rooms for a purpose unknown. Why would she wander about in a strange place? Vard rubbed the short stubble on his chin as he pondered the question. Why did Alecia ever wander about? She had found a mission and thought herself capable of the task. But what?

Vard checked his room but it was empty. How he wished he had his sword! He backed out of the room and crept along the hall to the stairs, descending to the ground floor and taking the passage to the garden. Perhaps she felt the need for peace. It was dark under the trees, but he had no need of extra light with his Defender-enhanced vision. He entered the garden and prowled around its margins, flicking quick glances toward the palace and the surrounding buildings. All was quiet. A half-moon provided weak light.

Acting on a hunch, he decided to check the outside walls of the building. He crossed back through the passage under the palace and emerged at the front, hiding in the shadows of a pillar as a pair of elves stalked past. Only his superior eyesight enabled him to see the soldiers before they spied him. He waited until they had moved on, then slipped across the front of the building below the windows and down a narrow alley that ran between Leth's residence and the next house. The crumbling masonry had been cleared from this side street, probably to aid in Leth's security. Vard flattened himself against the wall and scanned the passageway. There was no one in sight, nowhere to hide. He allowed his eyes to drift up the side wall of the palace and his stomach tightened, heart skipping a beat before thundering away.

A shadowy figure scaled the outside wall. The person inched along the stone, toward a darkened window, searching out toe and finger holds by feel. It was Alecia. Vard's heart pounded in his chest with fear for his princess. She was just a toehold from falling. If that aging masonry should crumble beneath her fingers or feet, it would be a crushing fall onto the hard stone of the alley. He held his breath and watched as she inched closer to her objective, her position so precarious he wasn't game to distract her. All he could hope for now was that she would gain the window without falling.

Her fingers gripped the stone frame. Vard forced himself to move silently down the alley to a position opposite, close enough to cushion Alecia's fall if needed, but further out of sight of the soldiers. His eyes never left her and his heart pounded loud in his ears. Time seemed to crawl as he watched her reach for the stone sill with her leading foot. Her body lurched and Vard heard a grunt as she slid toward the ground.

He threw himself forward in a desperate lunge and Alecia's body hit him, knocking the air from his chest. He lay unable to breathe for a long moment, Alecia unmoving on top of him. Two *Sis Lenweri* soldiers slid to a halt before him, one carrying a bow in his hand. The men hauled Alecia off him and Vard rolled over to cradle her head in his lap.

Though it was dark, he saw the arrow and blood pouring from a deep wound to Alecia's shoulder. The skin of her face was ashen as she looked up at him. Her lips moved.

"Don't try to talk, beloved."

Vard looked at the *Lenweri* who stood beside him. The man with the bow looked familiar, and scared. Vard had seen that shock before on the faces of soldiers after their first kill. "Get help, lad," he said. "She needs a healer."

The young *Lenweri* bolted but the older elf stood gazing down, arms folded across his chest. Vard seized the bottom of his robe and tore a strip from the hem. He packed it around the arrow in Alecia's back, but the blood continued to ooze freely from the wound, dripping onto his robe, the metallic smell stirring his Defender instincts. His heart had never beat this quickly in battle, his fear had never been this great. He could lose her. He licked dry lips and looked up at the *Lenweri*.

"That is a killing shot, kingdom man," the elf said, "a fine shot in the dark. What was the wench doing scaling the palace wall?"

Vard growled. "What does it matter? Do something, I can't lose her."

"Do something yourself. You kingdom men are soft to hang your life on a woman."

Alecia moaned and Vard murmured soothing words against her ear. Her face was white, her eyes closed. If help didn't come soon. . .

He tried to make her more comfortable, but she moaned again as the arrow brushed his thigh. He couldn't snap the shaft off. The shock might kill her. Instead he focused all his will on her recovery, noted the way her breathing turned fast and shallow, heard the rapid, panicked beat of her heart.

"Stand back man," a voice said from the darkness. Leth appeared, his robes sweeping the stone of the alley. He immediately dropped to the ground beside Alecia, one hand resting on her forehead, the other above her left breast. "She must not be moved until I can pull her back from the brink."

Vard felt a prickle up the nape of his neck as Leth muttered in the guttural language of the *Lenweri*. The sorcerer closed his eyes and Alecia screamed. It was the tortured scream of an animal.

Vard gripped Leth's shoulder and the man's eyes snapped open. "Whatever you're doing, stop!" he commanded. "You're killing her."

Leth sneered. "You ignorant pup! Get your hand off me if you wish her to live. Your interference is a distraction I don't need." Leth bent his head back to his task and closed his eyes. Alecia's screams resumed, her arms and legs thrashing against the hard stone.

Vard cushioned her limbs as much as he could without letting her head drop to the pavement but she would be sore if she survived. Leth didn't appear to think it important to protect Alecia's flailing extremities. He remained bent over her, his hands fixed to her chest and forehead.

After what seemed hours but must have been only seconds, Leth removed his hands from Alecia's body. Her screams died in one last, long shriek. Her breath came in ragged gasps, eyes closed, face paler than parchment. When Vard grasped her hands, they felt like ice.

"Will she live?"

"I was almost too late," Leth said. "I cannot say if she will live or die, but we must get her inside and warmed. I will have Failora prepare some broth." He turned to the Lenweri behind him. "Lift her."

Vard scooped Alecia into his arms and she moaned against his chest. At least the bleeding seemed to have stopped. "I'll take her to her room."

Now it was time for Leth to growl. "She is to be taken to my quarters. I will see to her care."

Vard frowned at his princess and swallowed the lump in his throat. He didn't want help from Leth but it was too late for that now. "I'll take her to your quarters but will remain." He spun and stalked back down the alley, Leth's footsteps and those of the soldier echoing on the stone behind him. The animal in him snarled at having the sorcerer at his defenseless back, but he had no choice but to trust he was safe for the moment. Leth had saved Alecia. Vard could tell she was improved, but what had those screams been about? It shouldn't take torture to heal and he was certain the agonized screams of his beloved had indicated true torment. Would he have been able to heal her if he had already come into his gift? He just didn't know the answer to that, and to so many questions.

They arrived at Leth's suite. The door swung open at a gesture from the sorcerer. "Failora! Pull back the blankets and stoke the fire. Then you must prepare healing broth. She is close to death."

"I thought you healed her," Vard snarled, laying Alecia on the huge bed and pulling the blankets over her.

Failora brought hot stones wrapped in blankets to lay at Alecia's feet. The woman seemed unsurprised at the turn of events, as though she attended bloodied patients every evening.

"I have done what I can for now," Leth said. "Her body can take no more of my ministrations. Perhaps if she survives the night I can try again tomorrow."

"I don't think I can let you perform your sorcery on her again," Vard said. "Her screams... it was torture."

"It is so every time I heal, especially when the flesh is penetrated by a weapon. See for yourself. The arrow is gone."

Leth crossed to the bed, gripped Alecia's tunic and shirt at the hole where the arrow had entered, and tore a larger rent in the fabric. A gaping hole marred the soft white flesh of her shoulder, but the shaft was indeed gone. Leth ran gentle fingers across Alecia's skin and she shivered. Vard closed his eyes and swallowed down the pang of jealousy the gesture evoked. He'd have to endure this for Alecia's sake but he wouldn't leave her side. At least then she might be safe. *Safe!* When had she ever been safe with him present?

Leth laid Alecia back against the pillows and covered her to the chin. Her breathing was fast and shallow, and where her skin had been pale before, now it was flushed. Leth frowned as he brushed his fingers across her cheek. "This is no good. She has lost much blood and yet her cheeks are aflame. I fear it signifies contamination of the wound."

Vard could not take his eyes from her. "She'll recover. She's strong." He looked at Leth and forced out the words he must say for the good of his lady. "I'm sorry for doubting you before. I see you've done what you can. Please continue to help her."

Leth frowned but Vard held his gaze. What convoluted plots did the wizard hatch inside his mind?

Finally Leth spoke. "Keep your apologies. I do not help Allandra as a favor to you, but for my own reasons. Stay with her or go, it doesn't matter to me either way. This night will be a long one." With those words, he swept across the room and out of the chamber.

Failora busied herself at a nearby table covered by a linen cloth. She poured measures of several colorful concoctions into a plain ceramic urn and stirred them with a gnarled stick. Smoke arose from the mixture as Failora stirred, and Vard's nose wrinkled as acrid fumes filled the room.

"Have a care, woman," he said. "You'll poison all of us instead of curing Allandra."

Failora spun to face him, her shawl falling to her elbows. "Who are you to come into my abode and treat me as a village woman?" she hissed. "I see the way you move, Anton. You think you own the world." She left her work and stepped closer to stare up into Vard's eyes. "You are nothing beside my master. He will grind you beneath his heel if you do not learn proper respect. I have seen him destroy better men than you."

Vard gazed down into the striking dark eyes of the elven woman. In another life he would have been drawn to her dark beauty, her lithe figure and passion. Now he had other concerns and other responsibilities. "Enough of your threats, woman, see to your patient." He retreated to a corner and settled himself on the floor, his eyes glued to the rise and fall of Alecia's chest. Failora spared him another glare and returned to her potion.

He couldn't predict what Leth's reaction to Alecia's adventure would ultimately be. For now the sorcerer seemed content to play healer, but what when she recovered? Leth couldn't ignore her behavior. Why could his beloved not simply act as most women would? Why must she fashion her own plans and act on them without his knowledge? He prayed to the Goddess this latest folly of Alecia's wouldn't take her life.

* * *

Awareness returned to Alecia, the crushing pain in her left shoulder forcing a moan through her dry lips. The mattress beneath her was lumpy and she was cold. The sharp scent of blood assailed her nostrils and fear sent cold tendrils through her stomach. She couldn't remember what had happened or where she was. The heavy gold brocade of the bed canopy greeted her hazy view as she cracked her eyes open. Even the muted light sent a searing stab through her temples. She closed her eyes, breathing deeply to overcome the nausea that threatened to swamp her.

"You're awake!" Vard's worried green eyes hovered above her. His hand reached for hers, his fingers gripping until they hurt. "I thought that. . . Never mind." He frowned, seeming lost for words. "What the devil were you doing scaling Leth's palace wall? Do you even know what occurred?"

Alecia's heart ached at the pain in Vard's voice. "I can't remember anything beyond dinner."

"I found you missing and went looking only to discover you about to climb into a window in this very chamber. One of his soldiers shot you and Leth has fought to save you." Vard's voice turned bitter. "It seems he's a healer as well. It was quite something to see."

"I feel so weak, Vard."

"As I suspected," Leth said, striding into the room, "you use a different name to that you've given me. I am glad to see you somewhat recovered. . . Allandra." He reached to place a hand on her forehead and Alecia flinched as energy radiated through her. It left her languid. "You will sleep now and when you wake you will need to eat." Fear and pain faded away and Alecia knew no more.

* * *

Vard swore as he returned to his room. The mood in Leth's chamber betrayed a tense waiting, an expectant menace, as though the axe would soon fall. The trouble was that Vard didn't know where the menace lay. So far he hadn't been called to account for Alecia's actions but that couldn't last. He stepped through the door and closed it, his eyes taking time to adjust to the darkness. Had he not left a roaring fire? That was several hours ago, but there should still be coals, surely? A prickle up the back of his neck gave a belated warning as an arm closed around his neck from behind.

"You will rue the day you ever entered *Elvandang*." The harsh whisper sounded in his ear and the arm tightened until Vard could barely speak. "I should kill you now and leave you to die wondering who bested you."

"Caele Aloe." Vard thought the voice belonged to the *Sis Lenweri* sergeant.

The man behind him hissed. "Perhaps what they say of you is true. You are kin with Leth. You must be to know my voice."

"What do you want with me," Vard growled, testing the strength of the arm about his neck. It tightened again sending Vard into a coughing fit.

"It would not be pleasant to die deprived of air, your throat crushed, would it kingdom man?"

"What's your problem, elf? I've done you no harm."

The arm tightened further and Vard's mind dimmed, the world slipping away. He gripped the stone at his neck, lurching toward the transformation. The bear would tear Caele Aloe limb from limb and Leth could pick up the pieces. A small voice wormed its way through his fuzzy brain. It latched a tendril of reason around the core of Vard that dwelt inside. He couldn't trust Leth to deal with this. The sorcerer would take advantage. He had already threatened to trap Vard in animal form and then Alecia would be at Leth's mercy.

He drew in a deep breath and with the last vestige of bear strength, rammed his elbow into Caele Aloe's upper stomach. There came a popping sound as of cartilage snapping and the elf flew backward into the door and slid to the floor. Vard continued to breathe deeply, feeling his muscles and mind come back to human form. The broken elf looked up at him, gasping for air.

"My son, my *only* son, has been called to account for his part in the wounding of your woman," Aloe croaked. "If he is found guilty, he will die."

Vard stared, believing the elf had lost his senses. "That can't be right. It's Alecia who trespassed." Too late, Vard realized he had used her real name, but Caele Aloe seemed not to notice.

"Tur loosed the arrow that brought her down. *Alen* Leth has decreed that Tur answer for the wounding of his guest." Grief swept across his features and Vard felt an answering sorrow. "He is but a boy of seventeen summers. I cannot lose him." The elf tried to rise but groaned and fell back to the stone floor. Drums sounded in the near distance and Vard looked a question at Aloe. The beat held a threat that pounded at Vard's gut.

"It is a call to trial," Caele Aloe said, reaching out his hand.

Vard helped him to his feet and the elf stood gasping for breath. "Take me to this trial."

Torches lit the dark faces of the *Lenweri* gathered in the huge clearing on the outskirts of the city of Amitania, known as *Elvandang* by the dark elves. It seemed all the *Lenweri* males and some of the women had turned out for the trial of Caele Aloe's son. A stone platform graced one end of the clearing, and Lord Leth was seated on a throne shaped from the trunk of a huge tree. The wood was golden and polished until it shone. Leth had changed from his robes of red and silver and was now garbed in white satin, strange symbols in crimson thread encircling the cuffs and neck of the robe. His head and hands were raised to the sky and his lips moved as though muttering a prayer.

Vard glanced at Caele Aloe and found the elf's fear-filled eyes on his son, who stood to one side on the stone platform. The young elf wore the traditional leggings and tunic of the *Lenweri* in colors of green and brown that matched the hues of their forest home. His eyes were wide as they met those of his father. Vard shook his head. There was something wrong here, something he was missing. None of this made sense. He made to walk forward and confront Leth but a group of large *Sis Lenweri* stepped in front of him and blocked his path. Caele Aloe snarled and also tried to push through the barrier but he was pulled to the side.

Vard had no choice but to allow the proceedings to take place unless he wanted to risk a transformation. As he watched, the light of a new day broke over the stone dais of the clearing, lighting the silver strands in the sorcerer's hair.

Leth lowered his arms, and his gaze swept the gathering, seeming to take in each individual. Despite himself, Vard was impressed.

"The first rays of the sun have caressed our home. It is time to pass judgment," the sorcerer said, his eyes on Tur Aloe. "This soldier wounded a guest of mine yester eve and her life still hangs in the balance. My honor is destroyed by this act and the accused must be called to account. The penalty is death by hanging. I will now give my decision."

Vard heard a shout from behind and turned to find Caele Aloe restrained on his back on the ground by a group of soldiers. The elf's face was red with his struggle to rid himself of his minders. "I must speak for my son. This is not right."

Vard knew he couldn't allow this trial to proceed, if trial it could be called. He raised his voice above the commotion behind him. "I ask leave to speak on behalf of the prisoner. Unlike most here, I was a witness. I believe there are extenuating circumstances."

Fury blazed from Leth's eyes. He really did like to be in complete control. "This is most irregular," he said, glaring at Vard. "Is my judgment not enough?"

"You wouldn't wish to kill an innocent man, Leth," Vard said. "Justice must prevail."

Absolute silence lay upon the clearing as Leth stared at Vard and then at the assembly. Finally he inclined his head. "Allow Anton to approach the dais."

Vard pushed his way through the *Sis Lenweri* to the stone platform. Suddenly he was glad of the gaudy robes that might enable him to stand on equal footing with Leth. He raised his arms and drew all eyes in the congregation. Two could play at this game. Behind him, the sorcerer's seething anger was tangible.

"People of the *Sis Lenweri*, I'm a stranger in your midst and I wouldn't presume to advise you how to conduct your trials. On this occasion I was present when the alleged offense occurred and believe I have something to offer."

Leth cleared his throat. "Do you deny your companion was injured by Tur Aloe last eve?"

Vard ground his teeth. "No, but—"

"Then what can there be to discuss? The boy is guilty of attempted murder. Let that be the end of the story."

"The injury happened in the performance of patrol duty."

"Agreed, but that is irrelevant in this case."

"How could it be irrelevant?" Vard could feel his ire rising. He had to keep calm. "He was protecting you. My companion was attempting to climb into a palace window."

A loud buzz swept the assembly at the revelation.

"Regardless, Tur Aloe should have applied more restraint. He has not taken enough care and it resulted in a near death and the loss of my honor. I say again, Anton, your intervention is irrelevant. Now be gone so I can pass sentence."

Caele Aloe wailed from his position on the ground, but Tur merely squared his shoulders and took a deep breath. It seemed he was prepared for whatever came, even death.

"This isn't right or just," Vard said, swallowing the torrent of words he wanted to utter.

"Be gone!"

At Leth's cry, guards grabbed Vard and pulled him off the dais and into the crowd. They stood around him, walling him in with hard muscle as angry muttering rippled through the crowd. The *Sis Lenweri* couldn't be happy that one of their own would die for an outsider.

"Tur Aloe, you caused grave injury to my guest and for that you are sentenced to hang until you are dead."

Caele's agonized scream sliced through Vard's composure, the pain of a father losing his only son. "You will die for this, Anton!"

It seemed Vard would be the easy target for this injustice, despite his efforts to rescue the boy. Tur was seized by his arms and marched away by two guards, stony expressions on his face and theirs. He didn't even spare a look for his father.

Caele was hauled to his feet, his face a ruin of tears and dirt. "You have made me dishonor myself and my son, kingdom man, and you have robbed my family of its heir. Hate is not a strong enough word for my feelings. I will see you dead."

"Take him somewhere to calm down," Leth said. "And do not allow him out until he swears to abide by my decision in peace."

The guards bowed and marched Caele Aloe away, the dark elf's shoulders slumped as if all the fight had left him. Vard felt a deep sadness at the waste of a young life that could so easily have been spared. But he had done what he could, and there was another purpose for his presence here. He couldn't risk further endangering his relationship with Leth, lest the sorcerer send him away before he had learned all he could. Still, allowing Tur Aloe to hang went against every Defender ideal he knew. Obviously Leth hadn't embraced this aspect of his heritage. He met the anger in Leth's eyes and gave a faint bow of his head before leaving the clearing.

CHAPTER 9

ALECIA'S eyes opened to bright sunshine, through the window near the bed. A worm of unease squirmed in her gut at waking in the lord's bed, no matter how ill she had been. Failora sauntered through and Alecia admired the woman's dark beauty as she tidied the room. She glided up to the bed and laid her hand on Alecia's brow.

"You were gravely ill last eve," she said. "I did not know if his powers would be equal to the task of saving your life."

"Lord Leth saved me?"

Failora inclined her head. "He is a great healer. He will visit shortly to speak with you. You must be honest with him. It is the only way." She left the room and returned with a covered tray, which she laid on Alecia's lap. "Eat everything and you will soon be strong."

Alecia's stomach grumbled at the aromas issuing from under the cloth. "Where is Vard… Anton?"

Failora's eyes narrowed but she said nothing of the slip. "He was here earlier, but then had to be about his business. He will check on you after lunch. Eat."

Alecia flicked the cover off the tray and examined its contents. There appeared to be soup, crusty bread, and milk. Probably goat's milk. She wrinkled her nose as she sniffed the pungent goblet but knew she must drink it for her babe's sake. At the thought, a deep dread swept over her and cold filled her core. She raised the goblet with trembling fingers. What if her accident had harmed the babe? How stupid could she be? Her free hand crept over her abdomen hoping to feel something that would tell her if her baby still lived.

"You are very pale, Allandra," a deep voice said from the doorway. Lord Leth stood there, his eyes narrowed, looking directly at the hand on her stomach. "How do you feel?"

"I am well, My Lord," she said. "Thank you for what you did last night. In the circumstances, it's more than I deserved."

"I beg to differ, my dear," he said, walking to the bed and seating himself on the edge beside her.

Alecia slid her hand from her belly and picked up a piece of bread. "I'm sorry for my actions last night. I don't know what came over me."

"I'm beginning to put the pieces together, despite the deception you have practiced." His eyes flared golden in the shadow under the bed's canopy, and fear squirmed in Alecia's gut. "Your companion is Vard Anton, former captain in Prince Zialni's Army. Last eve I heard you call him Vard. Of course, we have heard whispers of the scandal that has engulfed Brightcastle and the Kingdom of Thorius, even as far north as this. A captain of the royal army disgraced and on the run with the prince's daughter. That would be you, Princess Alecia Allandra Dosodra Zialni."

Alecia closed her eyes, her heart racing, and prayed to the Goddess that this news wouldn't end in danger. Leth had the gleam of the predator in his eyes, and her heart beat faster when she thought of the ways in which he could use the information. But it was no use denying his words. "You're correct in your deductions." Her voice was faint, her arms weak. If only she could disguise her pregnancy for some time to come.

Leth favored her with a warm smile and reached to remove the bread roll before kissing her fingers. "I am delighted to make your acquaintance, Princess. Now I am doubly glad my ministrations have been successful. I will see that no further harm befalls you."

Vard pushed through the door and strode toward the bed. The hair at his temples was sweaty, and a film of dust lay on his tunic and breeches.

"What has occurred here? What's amiss, Allandra?" His anxious eyes flicked from Leth to her as he stood on the balls of his feet, primed for a fight.

"I was just leaving, Anton. I will allow the princess to tell you of our conversation. Until this evening." He left, an amused smile playing across his tanned features.

"So he knows," Vard said, a frown creasing his brow.

"He's no idiot." Alecia covered her stomach with her hand. Perhaps Leth hadn't discerned her pregnancy during his healing. Or maybe she really had lost the babe.

Vard noticed the movement. "Are you in pain?"

"No, merely hungry." She frowned as she returned to her meal. "I wonder what this means for our stay here."

"The man who shot you is now dead. Leth ordered his hanging."

She froze, swallowing down bile that threatened to flood her throat. "How has this come to pass?"

Vard related his experience with Caele Aloe and the trial. "The execution took place shortly after. Caele Aloe is in prison until he comes to terms with the death of his son. My heart breaks for his loss, but we're in danger."

"We can't leave, Vard. You need Lord Leth."

He frowned; his gaze clouded with uncertainty. Her fierce leader didn't know the best course to take.

"I need Leth, but my instinct tells me he'll use this knowledge of us. I fear you'll be hurt. You're a princess of the realm. There's no end to the ways he could exploit that."

"I'll manage, Vard. I'm tough and have survived lecherous old men before."

Vard's eyes blazed with anger. "Leth is a sorcerer and a Defender! You're no match for him. Keep your distance until I discover if he can teach me what I need to learn. If he can't, we must flee at the earliest opportunity."

"Granted, beloved. I'll avoid the lord, but I can't do that while I rest in his bed."

Heat seared her cheeks at the thought of what might occur if the sorcerer cast his enchantments on her. She could only too well imagine his arms around her, his lips on her skin. She might well be powerless to stop his advances, for he'd have no scruples in using his talents against her. She sighed, appalled at the position she had again fallen into. At least Vard was with her this time and she had her babe to think of. If the babe still survived. A wave of sadness and fear made tears well in her eyes.

Vard took her into his arms. His lips caressed her hair and his hands rubbed her back. "I'll find a way to protect you." She took a deep breath and closed her eyes, inhaling the musky scent that was all Vard. She drew back and looked into his eyes.

"I know you wish to protect me, but you can't do that if you leave me," she said, her voice more than a little accusing. She would fight for him in any way she could. "You still plan to dump me at some farm thinking your nearness is a threat."

"I'll protect you in whatever way I can. If that means leaving you alone, so be it. You know it would destroy me to be the instrument of your death. How many times must I threaten your life for you to understand?"

"How many times must I repeat that without you I may as well be dead? Tell me where I'm safest for I don't know. I choose to be with you, to have your arms around me and feel the brush of your lips on my skin." She simply couldn't allow Vard to walk out of her life believing she would be better off.

Vard rose from the bed and stalked across to the very window Alecia had tried to enter the evening before. She watched the play of emotions across his face and wished he could confide what he held in his heart.

"Tell me what troubles you." She tried to swivel in the bed and the movement caused a stabbing pain that left her sick to her stomach.

Vard had closed his eyes and leant with his hands either side of the window.

"I want to understand your pain," she said, "but you never talk of your past."

He drew a deep breath and turned to face her. "Perhaps this is what it will take to convince you that I'm a danger. Perhaps then you won't be so glad to spend time in my company."

She glared at him. "Nothing could ever turn me against you." Especially not if she carried his child.

He laughed but the sound held no amusement. "When I was a young boy, I had no brothers or sisters. My mother had a difficult time bringing me into the world and eventually died of birthing complications several months later. I can't remember her, but my father was crushed. He and I were close but there was always sadness in his eyes when he looked at me. I thought the melancholy came from seeing his son grow up without a mother."

Alecia listened with rapt attention, soaking up the words that seemed to pour from Vard's soul.

"In an attempt to give me the siblings I never had, Father encouraged my cousin Frel – his brother's only son and a boy of similar age – to spend time with me. We were more like brothers than cousins. With Frel, I learned to wrestle and shoot a longbow and to hunt. They were good days but I was uneasy. As I moved toward manhood, strange feelings began to arise. My senses became more acute. I could smell deer and rabbit from miles away and my vision was almost as good. Frel noticed and joked about the curse of our family. Our generation of Antons was the one destined to produce a freak who would turn into an animal and go mad.

"I laughed at Frel but when I peered into the rivers, I began to see strange gold flecks in my eyes. Father started refusing to look at me and the fear in him grew. I didn't understand then but it was my Defender gift rearing its ugly face. One day when we were hunting together, Frel and I were running through the forest chasing a boar when the thing turned on us. It was the largest pig I'd ever seen and it charged right at me. I can still hear Frel's scream. That's the last I remember except for jumbled images from a nightmare. Only it wasn't a nightmare. I awoke in the forest, blood splashed all over myself and the grass nearby. The boar was dead, appearing as though a large creature had feasted upon it. Only the skull remained intact. Frel's crumpled body lay mangled on a rock nearby."

Vard closed his eyes again and clutched the stone windowsill. As Alecia watched, his nails left gouges in the stone. He had killed his own cousin. No wonder he hated his Defender persona. No wonder he feared to be alone with her.

Self-loathing swamped Vard. He opened his eyes to the crumbling wall of the building across the alley and swallowed down fear so acute it paralyzed him. He hated himself, for what he was and for what he had done. At times he lay awake, pondering the crimes he had committed, as the wolf or the bear, that he had no knowledge of. How many victims really lay in his wake? One thing he did know; he couldn't afford to number Alecia amongst them.

He squared his shoulders and turned to face the woman who had stolen his heart. Her eyes were large, as if she were seeing him for the first time. Vard the killer, the animal who murdered his own kin.

"What happened then?" she asked.

He frowned. "What do you mean 'what happened then'? This is no fairy story to be told at a child's bedside. This is real." He couldn't make his voice softer, couldn't suppress the anger.

Alecia flinched, and shame washed over him at the sudden spike of unease in her scent.

"What did you do when you discovered your cousin?" she asked.

"I panicked. I had only transformed once before and was so spooked by the experience I told no one. I didn't understand what I was. I thought I was a monster, the monster from Frel's stories, the freak of the family. Poor Frel, he should've known better than to befriend me." Memory of his cousin's shredded flesh flashed through his mind and he hid his face in his hands. "For hours, I sat there shaking. Finally it grew dark and the creatures of the forest began to sniff around, the scavengers. I knew I had to remove Frel's body so I took it back to my home and left it on the doorstep. Then I ran. Deep into the forest, never intending to return, not knowing what I had become."

"Vard," Alecia said, her voice barely a whisper, "you're not a monster. You know what you are now and will master your gift."

"Gift! Father found Frel's body the next morning and knew what had befallen him - and me. He buried Frel and said nothing to his brother. Frel's family still believes he and I perished in the forest." Vard's voice broke. "Father came looking for me, not knowing what he'd find. I'll always love him for that. He found me in a cave, miles away, and kept me hidden while he tried to teach me my heritage, but he wasn't a Defender himself and his father hadn't shared much with him before he died. There was little he could do to help but he gave me the amber stone, which had belonged to my grandfather. With the stone, I learned how to control the transformation to a degree. Eventually, I was able to visit Father in his cabin and I'd come at night to see him. He became increasingly withdrawn until one night he didn't answer. The cabin was empty and I haven't seen him since."

* * *

Alecia felt numb at the reality that was Vard's past. The slaughter of his cousin, the self-loathing, the pain of deceit that had been shared by his father. Imagine the guilt of covering up something as tragic as the slaughter of a nephew! Each sentence had revealed a hurt even greater than the last.

"I don't know how you live with the pain," she said, her voice merely a whisper in the room.

"I have no choice, dearest, but I hope you can now understand why I'm so afraid of hurting you."

She nodded, still lost in the story of a young man taken over by the beast within.

"We must get you moved from here," he said, lifting her off Leth's bed. Pain shot through her left shoulder and she gritted her teeth to stop from crying out as Vard carried her back to her room. She was sick to the stomach by the time he deposited her on her bed. He pulled the furs up and adjusted her pillows. His gold-green eyes studied her.

"You've gone pale. I'm sorry," he said, smoothing the hair from her face. "I'll see if I can find a draught for the pain."

Alecia's heart broke that he could blame himself in any way. This was all her fault. "Don't be sorry, beloved. I'd be grateful for a sleeping potion." She feared nightmares without something. Vard's story had upset her and she knew she would see visions of torn flesh should she be allowed to sleep naturally.

He stared at her for a moment longer, his expression bleak, before brushing her cheek with his fingers and leaving the room.

She sighed and settled back on the pillows, the throbbing in her shoulder a painful reminder of her stupid brush with death. She had learned nothing and now Leth knew almost everything, perhaps already did know everything. She had no knowledge of whether he was skilled enough to discern a pregnancy. If he knew, she was in danger twice over. Leth would use the babe to further his ambitions somehow, and Vard would leave her if he suspected his presence endangered a child. Or would he? Perhaps knowing he was a father would tie him to her side. What father wouldn't stay to care for his child?

A father who thought the child and the mother would be better off without him. A father who put the safety of his family first. Vard was such a man.

Alecia closed her eyes as she waited for the potion, praying there was still a child within her womb for Vard to love.

CHAPTER 10

VARD slammed his fist down on the stone edge of the parade ground fountain and a section of the coping crumbled. The late morning sun bounced off the shards of stone as they floated in the water before sinking.

"Damn Leth! The bastard is leading me on." He closed his eyes, gripping the amber stone on the leather cord around his neck. When would he achieve control? He was no further along one month after arriving in Amitania than he had been at the beginning. Lessons with Leth had been sporadic and when they occurred, the sorcerer insisted Vard not use his amulet to aid his control. But what if the amber stone was essential for his Defender skills? His grandfather had been in possession of the talisman so perhaps Vard's gift required a focus such as this. All he knew was that he had made almost no headway while his frustration grew daily.

The sorcerer also refused to confirm or deny that healing was a part of the defender gift though Vard suspected he had some talent there. He felt an affinity for sick and injured people. Alecia had needed something constructive to do once she recovered and had volunteered her services at the hospital. She visited every day and had taken him on several tours of the infirmary. Vard thought he could see auras around the ill that corresponded to their sickness. Crimson for inflammation, blue for diseases of the mind, yellow if there was disease of the belly, infection showed as green and fractures of the bones were a sickly combination of purple, crimson and green.

He had tried laying his hands on the heads of the infirm and concentrating on their ills but so far nothing had occurred beyond strange looks. It amused Alecia, but she readily admitted Vard's talent might be useful for diagnosing complaints. When Vard questioned Leth, he had been evasive, and he never let Vard witness any of the healing he undertook unless it was with potions.

Vard felt a growing need to be away from the city of crumbling stone. His training of the soldiers was progressing well. Many had fashioned longbows and learned how to shoot them. Swordplay was rapidly becoming the contest of the day, but the one resident who had declined to fight Vard was Leth himself. The fact that he couldn't gauge Leth's fighting prowess nagged at Vard. He knew little more about Leth than he had the first day.

The sorcerer had an agenda all of his own, that was obvious. And those plans included Alecia. To add more mystery to the situation, Leth was often away for days at a time and on each return, the smiles he granted Vard were more smug, those to Alecia more calculating. Yes, they needed to be free of Leth's influence as soon as he could arrange it.

Alecia approached, fear swamping her favorite lavender perfume. Vard's heart thumped an answering rhythm as he greeted her. "What's the matter?" he said, taking her hands in his.

"That's Ramón's horse," she said, her wide eyes following a black gelding as he was led past by a *Lenweri* soldier. A spike of jealousy struck Vard at the mention of the man who had recently lusted after the princess. Squire Ramón Zorba worked for Prince Zialni and had been the last person they saw before fleeing Brightcastle. Vard would be happy if he never set eyes on the man again but, if Alecia's tone was anything to go by, she still cared deeply for Zorba.

The black horse had his ears back and as Vard watched, he struck at the elf, teeth bared, just missing his handler's arm.

"Perhaps it is." Vard turned back to her.

"I tell you, it's his," she said, her voice low and urgent. "Arrow is a bad-tempered beast. How else does a *Sis Lenweri* come to have his mount unless it was taken in battle? I must know if Ramón is well."

Vard frowned. "He might have sold it, or even if he has battled the *Lenweri*, many horses bolt and are captured by the enemy. It doesn't mean the squire was hurt or killed."

"But it might!" Alecia started past him, heading to where the horse had disappeared into the stable.

"Stay away from it," Vard muttered beneath his breath. "No good will come of you asking about that horse. They won't tell you where he came from or what happened to his rider. Just leave it alone." She had that stubborn set to her mouth that spelled trouble. "Please."

She stiffened and Vard prepared for an argument, but then her shoulders slumped. "You're right, I suppose. We must tread warily. But I'd give anything to know how the elves came by that horse. Ramón would lose his right hand before he'd let Arrow be taken. I can't help but fear for him."

"There's nothing you can do for him now," Vard said, struggling to keep his voice level. "You look tired. Have a rest and I'll meet you for dinner. There are matters to which I must attend."

Alecia kissed his cheek and left without further argument. She did look tired, and increasingly so with every day. She worked too hard in the hospital. There was always someone to care for, and growing numbers of soldiers with battle wounds. But it wasn't only the hospital that caused Alecia's tiredness. Vard suspected she lay awake at night, worrying. He had taken to sleeping in his own bed, afraid he'd transform in his sleep and hurt her. The enchantment had worn off the amulet and any anger, frustration, fear or arousal could push him over the edge. Only it was worse now because Leth had increased the irritation and rage building inside him. He suspected he was being used, and that Leth was deliberately goading him toward a situation where he could be dispensed with; when he had completed the training of the army, of course!

Vard shook his head. This state of affairs was intolerable but he couldn't see what to do about it. The arrival of Ramón's horse did confirm one thing. Kingdom men were coming up against dark elves in battle, or at least skirmishes, and Vard was almost certain his training was aiding their cause.

CHAPTER 11

ALECIA waited for Vard in her chamber. Their meal had been delivered and lay cooling. Wind through the crack of a window that wouldn't close made her shiver. Vard was always late for meals now and she hated the growing distance between them. They hadn't slept together for over three weeks and desire raged through her whenever she saw him or thought of him. If they didn't couple soon, she'd explode. Perhaps it was her pregnancy that made her so eager for him. Alecia smiled at the thought of the babe within. She was so lucky she hadn't lost her precious cargo after the injury six weeks ago.

She turned as Vard entered the room. He had removed his tunic and washed his face and hands. He looked tired. Perhaps his sleep was as broken as hers?

"The dinner cools, beloved," she said, walking to him and kissing him full on the lips, pressing her body to his. She felt him stir and then he gently pushed her away.

He sat, so she followed his lead.

"I missed you at luncheon," she said.

"I ate with the soldiers. How was your day?"

She sighed. They sounded so stiff and formal. She had never dreamed it would be like this between them. "Hospital duties, as usual, though I did have an interesting conversation with a young soldier today. He told me of the raid that resulted in his brother's death. This boy participated as well. It was an ambush on a small convoy heading east toward Wildecoast."

Vard looked up, suddenly interested. "When?"

"Around six weeks ago. Their troop was scattered, and it has taken over a month for him to make his way back here. He told of a golden-haired man on a black horse who was the leader of this convoy, and of a woman traveling in a carriage. It has to be Ramón." Alecia suddenly felt homesick for Brightcastle even though there was nothing for her back there. But Ramón would always be dear to her. He simply had to be alive and well. "Why do you suppose he was traveling to Wildecoast with winter threatening?"

Vard frowned. "I think there's something I should tell you. It may have no relation to your news, but perhaps it will."

Alecia's heart started to pound. *Oh Goddess, what is he about to tell me?* She clutched his hand across the table. "Is he dead?"

"I've no news of Ramón. This pertains more to your father." He paused as if searching for words.

"Tell me, Vard!"

He took a deep breath and swallowed hard. "Your father has advertised for a bride. It may well be the squire is involved in this in some way."

Alecia's stomach knotted. "Father is to marry?"

"He may already be married by now."

"And how do you know this?"

"Hetty told me."

"But you saw her nearly two months ago. Did you not think to tell me?"

Vard remained silent.

He had not told her that her father was to marry? That he was to dishonor the memory of his first wife by replacing her? "Why didn't you tell me?" she repeated.

"I decided not to because I didn't want you returning to Brightcastle to 'fix' things. Hetty advised you should stay away as well."

"You should've told me."

"Perhaps."

"I'm not some weak girl to be pampered and cared for by her man. I deserved the truth."

"You're right. I should've told you, but I knew it would hurt you to think of your mother being replaced, and by a younger woman. He seeks an heir."

"Of course it hurts to think of Mama being replaced, but it hurts more to know you lied to me. What else have you withheld?"

Vard's gaze slid away.

"There *is* something else!" Alecia stood and her chair fell backward. She leaned over the table, her hands bunched into fists at her side. "What is it?"

He met her eyes. "Finus."

Alecia's gut knotted and she felt giddy. But she must face this news. Better to know than to wonder. "What of him?"

"Hetty believes he *was* mortally wounded the night we fled the castle, even though palace rumors tell of a recovery. Your friend says it's a matter of time before the lord is dead. He may already be bones in the grave."

Relief flooded her. How good it felt not to have that shadow looming over her. She righted her chair and sat, her mind whirling through the consequences of all she had learned. "I'm free to return."

"You can't be sure Finus is dead."

"I must know, Vard. I must know it all: Ramón, my new stepmother, my people. I must know how they all fare. It's my responsibility."

Vard's gaze was hard upon her but she refused to back down.

"This is exactly why I didn't tell you," he said, "because you would throw caution to the wind and charge back to Brightcastle to right all the wrongs. It's what led you into disaster last time."

"That disaster brought us together!"

"You know what I mean!"

"Do I?"

"You haven't changed, Alecia. Need I remind you that your meddling has nearly killed you at least twice? You have no care for your own safety."

"I've heard enough! You can't protect me from the world and you must not lie to me for any reason." The thought of the child within gave her a sharp stab of guilt but she plowed on. "You don't sleep with me anymore. You seem to want no intimate contact, and now I find you're withholding information about my family. You have no right."

Vard stood. "I have every right. While you're with me you're my responsibility."

"I'm my own woman and have my own duty – to my people. You can't protect me from that. Swear you'll tell all in future." She refused to listen to the voice that told her she wanted it all her own way; to pick and choose what Vard needed to know while she demanded to know it all. But it was her babe and its future at stake. That was different. An innocent child must be protected, and if she told Vard the truth, her child might never have the chance to know his father.

"I can't do that, and you won't change my mind no matter how you argue. I kept that information from you for your own good and will do so again if I must." He paused, his eyes wounded, his jaw tight. He gave her a small bow. "I'm tired and so will take my leave. I wish you a restful night."

Alecia stared at Vard's retreating form, unable to believe he had rebuffed her. He had changed from the loving man of two months ago, and it had all begun with their arrival in Amitania. Perhaps he was right and Leth was only using Vard to steer him toward certain disaster. How were they ever to escape Leth's clutches and what would be their fate if they did? Change was afoot in the kingdom and Alecia had her part to play, but not from the ruins of Amitania. Somehow, she must rise above this and resume her rightful place. But to do that, she must know more. It seemed Vard wouldn't help her in that particular endeavor.

* * *

Two weeks after Vard gave Alecia the news of her father and Finus, he stood watching the *Sis Lenweri* longbow men going through their drills. He had to admire their skill after only two months of training, but they were a strong people with uncannily long vision so perhaps it shouldn't be surprising.

Leth appeared at his elbow. "I came to advise you I'll be leaving tonight and gone for several days, Anton. Make good use of your time while I'm away."

Vard stopped himself from showing his surprise by the barest margin. Damn, the man could sneak up on him as no other could.

His mentor smiled the oily smile that made Vard's gut boil.

Vard frowned. Why tell him this time? "I always use my time wisely, *Alen* Leth." He wouldn't ask the purpose of this trip. It would do no good. He opened his mouth to broach the subject of Leth's mentorship, then thought better of it. If Leth knew Vard was discontent, he might keep closer watch on them. "Have a good trip."

Leth nodded and swept away in a flurry of black and silver robes. Vard watched him go, musing on the deep and convoluted mind of his mentor. He snorted in disgust. The man was no one's teacher. He waited until the sorcerer was clear of the training ground then stalked after him in search of Alecia.

* * *

Alecia squeezed cool water from the cloth and lay it back on the forehead of the soldier she tended. "Rest easy, soldier. It's but a scratch. You'll heal in no time." She hid her frown from the young elf. Too many had died of "scratches" lately. If only she could discern the ill that caused the deaths… But so far they had always occurred when Lord Leth was absent, and it seemed he was the only one who might understand what was happening and how they could be healed.

There was a scrape at the door, and she looked up to find Vard staring at her, an unreadable expression on his face. "Come, Vard," she said. He moved close to her and she stood on tiptoes to whisper in his ear. "What is the aura you see around that young *Lenweri*? He isn't recovering and I haven't been able to determine what ails him."

Vard stared at the patient. "Two auras surround him," he said. "One is crimson, and the other sickly green."

"Infection," she said, "just like the others." *But how and why?* "Never mind, perhaps Lord Leth can be called."

"I wouldn't count on it," he said. "He's leaving for another of his trips today."

She frowned. "I'd be much happier if I knew where he went and the purpose of these trips."

"We won't have to worry much longer. I'll secure our horses and we'll leave before he returns. It's the perfect opportunity." He looked around as if fearful of being overheard. "Meet me in my room and we'll talk of it."

Vard left and Alecia completed her checks on the last patient, washed her hands, and followed him out.

* * *

Vard had packed his belongings by the time Alecia arrived at his chambers. The thought of life on the road sent shivers over the base of her skull. Her pregnancy had survived her shooting, but would it survive living rough? She needed good food, not to be jostled around in a saddle day after day. Unwilling, her hands closed over her belly and then dropped away. She mustn't draw attention to her swelling abdomen or Vard really would leave her. So far, she had been lucky and crafty enough to conceal the pregnancy, but she had caught Leth's eyes on her abdomen of late. He suspected her condition, even if Vard did not.

"Must we run again?" she said, her voice weary.

"You're fully recovered, Alecia. As fit as I've ever seen you. I'm learning nothing from Leth and the longer we stay the more opportunity we give him to use us."

Alecia frowned. She couldn't disagree with his words but every step they took away from Amitania would be a step toward her life without Vard. "At least here there is still hope that you can master your Defender gifts.

"Damn it, Alecia, the man has taught me little in two months except frustration. As each day goes by, I come nearer to losing it in his presence. He goads me and says his purpose is to provide provocation so I can master my temper and control the transformation." He raked his fingers through his hair and Alecia wrapped her arms around herself.

"I can't even sleep with you for fear that I'll transform in my dreams and you'll be dead before I awake, before you awake! The sorcerer isn't helping, he's manipulating us, and I can't take it any longer."

"And so, I've no choice but to follow where you lead?" She couldn't suppress the bitterness she felt.

Vard's eyes hardened. "You're a free woman and can go where you will."

They stared at each other in silence for long moments. She noticed a deep fear in his eyes; the same fear that was always there, lurking in the background, but stronger since he had related the story of his cousin's death. She knew he regretted exposing himself, and two months of life in Amitania hadn't caused the fear to fade. It was weeks since they had coupled and the distance between them pained her more than she could express. That he could even suggest she'd stay when he left… She dropped her eyes to the crimson runner on the stone floor.

"It was merely *my* frustration talking, beloved," she said. "I'll prepare for our departure." Some way must be found for them to renew the love that had brought them together. Perhaps if she told him of their child? *No!* She would tell him when she had to and not before. She turned to leave.

"Alecia," he said, taking two steps toward her. "I know you've found a purpose here, but Leth threatens us and I must continue my search for a mentor. Already we've stayed too long. Go to your room and pack, and remember we travel lightly."

He turned away and she stared at his stiff shoulders, longing to throw her arms around him, to feel his hard length against her soft curves, to hear her name on his lips. She left, not knowing how to bridge the distance between them.

CHAPTER 12

I‍T WAS dark in the hall when they stepped from her room. Vard's hand was hot around hers as he led her to the stairs. They descended in silence, both clothed in dark elven breeches and tunics, their weapons slung about them. Vard had ventured out earlier, when most *Sis Lenweri* had been at dinner, and retrieved their horses. He wouldn't say if he had injured anyone in the process. Alecia's days of killing mercenaries seemed far in her past and she had no wish to be associated with murder and killing any more. Perhaps it was the life growing inside that had brought about the change.

They crept through the dark streets following the path Vard had mapped out after weeks of examining patrol routes. Alecia had wondered how he didn't go cross-eyed as he studied the convoluted paths the *Sis Lenweri* patrols used. He swore to her the path they now took was the least frequented route out of Amitania. Her gut froze at the thought of traversing the depths of the forest once they did leave the city's outskirts. The last two months had done nothing to diminish the sense of foreboding the forest, with its huge trees and thick fog, evoked within her. They'd be crossing at least some of it during darkness.

But first they must evade the city patrols. As the thought entered her head, Vard dragged her into a doorway just in time to dodge a patrol of six soldiers as they stalked by. Even in the darkness they had a grace to rival Vard's. Her breath quickened and her heart hammered as the last of the elves disappeared. She sagged against a wooden doorframe, but Vard dragged her back into the alley and on toward the outskirts of Amitania.

Alecia tried to pry her hand from Vard's, but he held it like a vice. Already she felt the need to rest. She opened her mouth to ask if they could take a small break but a tall *Sis Lenweri* appeared on the street in front of them. It was Caele Aloe.

"The kingdom man and his *woman*," Aloe hissed, coming up onto his toes and brandishing a sword. "How fitting you should die this night by my sword, the weapon you helped me master."

Vard drew his own sword from its scabbard. "I have no wish to harm you, Aloe. Step aside and let us leave."

"I have watched you closely since my release, hiding my anger and need for revenge. I see things the others don't, even *Alen* Leth. Your horses are missing from the stable, but I have discovered them."

Alecia's heart lurched anew at the words and her hand came to her mouth to stifle a gasp. What if he had removed the horses?

Caele Aloe's eyes latched onto Alecia's in the dark. "Yes, kingdom wench, you will never find your horses without me. But do not fear. I will dispose of your companion and claim you for my own. I will make a new life with you somewhere far away. There is nothing to keep me in *Elvandang*."

Alecia swallowed and gripped Vard's sleeve. He gave his head a small shake and she removed her hand. He couldn't fight with her hanging off his arm.

"I ask again, *Gir* Aloe, that you step aside." Vard's voice held a ring of command but it fell upon deaf ears.

Caele Aloe snarled and hurled himself at Vard, their swords clashing. Alecia flung herself out of the way, flattening against the wall behind her, eyes riveted to the scene. The elf was a formidable opponent. He had fought Vard many times over the last month and she had witnessed some of the matches. His skill had steadily increased and now Alecia knew what had driven him. *Revenge.* A tendril of fear curled around her stomach. He couldn't best Vard, could he?

The men moved back and forth, attacking and defending in turns, their movements graceful. The light of mad determination lit Caele Aloe's elfin eyes, but Vard appeared more frantic as the moments passed. It was as if he was pushing to end the fight quickly, while the elf danced round him, intent on dragging the contest out. As the minutes ticked by, Alecia began to fear discovery. They had everything to lose, while Aloe had already lost everything dear to him. It made for a dangerous opponent.

Vard staggered and went down on one knee. His gleeful challenger squealed as he moved in for the kill, raising his sword for a blow that would have taken Vard's head from his shoulders. Vard ducked, pivoted and ran his sword through Aloe's gut, the gleaming metal spearing right through the elf. Aloe's squeal became a gurgle as he fell forward, and Vard twisted his blade free of the body. He was dead before he hit the ground. Vard stayed where he was, kneeling in the dirt of the alley, his chest rising and falling, the dark no cover for his grim visage.

They had no time for reflection as footfalls sounded, coming closer.

Vard pushed himself to his feet, cleaned his sword on Aloe's tunic and grabbed Alecia's hand.

* * *

The *Sis Lenweri* patrol was right behind them and Alecia's strength had run out. She would have been left behind long ago were it not for Vard. His hand engulfed hers and gave her courage. He pulled them into a narrow passage, a footpath between streets, and turned to face her.

"We can't outrun them like this," he said, looking deep into her eyes. She could see nothing of his expression. "I'll become the wolf. You must ride, just as you did when fleeing your father's castle."

Her mind flashed back to that night, saw again the gigantic black wolf and remembered the feel of his strong legs beneath her. Could she face that again? They froze as the soldiers pelted past their hideout.

"Quickly, they'll soon back track to find us. I must have your answer."

She nodded and he handed his bow and arrows to her. She slung them about her person, anything to distract herself from what she was about to witness. Vard closed his eyes and gripped the amber stone at his throat. His outline blurred, swelling and shrinking, as his human limbs and clothes morphed into the body of the wolf. A low growl came from deep in his throat as his golden eyes swiveled to hers. She thought her heart could beat no faster, but she had been wrong. The steady gaze of the wolf pushed it to new limits and her hands closed protectively over her stomach. It couldn't be good for her babe to know such fear.

She felt frozen in place and time, but the huge creature whined and shuffled his shoulder against her, and she came out of her trance. Grunting with the effort, she hoisted herself and their weapons onto the broad shoulders of the wolf. They turned to retrace their steps only to find the way blocked by a dozen elven soldiers. They seemed stunned to find a woman astride a creature from nightmare, but their surprise didn't last long. With a blood-curdling cry, the leader launched himself forward, already raising his short bow, and the others followed.

Alecia's body was ripped around as the wolf spun and hurled himself in the opposite direction, the passage barely wide enough to accommodate them. Something sliced past her head and she ducked, sending a fervent prayer to the Goddess to spare her another injury. She didn't think her body or mind could bear the penetration of sharp metal again. Her knees brushed the stone on one side and she squeezed her legs inward. Vard growled beneath her. More arrows flew past and Alecia crouched even lower, the movement threatening to send her legs into the walls.

In a bound they were clear of the passage and in a broad street. Vard immediately took another wider passage off the street and threaded his way in a zigzag pattern through the outskirts of Amitania, at a dead run. She lost count of the turns and of the boulders and stones that rose up at them out of the darkness. She prayed for salvation and thanked the Goddess for Vard's night vision.

With a last bound, the enormous black wolf cleared a fallen column, that had once been part of the wall of Amitania, and sped right along the fortification. Alecia's tired mind puzzled over how the wolf still knew where to find the horses. Or did he? And even if they found the hiding spot, would the horses still be there? She twisted her fingers in his pelt in frustration and fear, and the creature whined.

"I'm sorry, my fine steed. I didn't mean to hurt you," she whispered, her body crouched over his shoulder. His fierce eye flicked toward her.

Before long, they turned left into the forest, and Alecia scanned the passing trees, expecting ambush. If Caele Aloe had acted alone, they might be safe for now. Even without horses, Vard could carry her to safety as the wolf. Or could he? How long could he remain the wolf? Hadn't he said there were risks in transformation? What would she do if he became trapped in that form? As the thought slammed into her mind, her mount slowed to a trot and took a narrow track into the forest. Moments later a clearing with two saddled horses came into view.

Alecia had only seconds to feel relief before both horses screamed and pulled back on their tethers, eyes rolling wildly. She slid from the wolf's back and flung herself at the horses. They couldn't afford to lose their mounts. She had only taken two steps before she was hauled backward out of the clearing, the wolf's jaws tugging on her cloak. In the end she fell onto her back and the wolf planted a huge paw on her chest and licked her face. His hot breath caressed her cheek and she froze, not understanding what was happening.

Vulnerable under the mass of hard sinew and muscle, she locked eyes with the creature. It took her breath away. Her heart thudded anew and her mouth lost all moisture. This wasn't Vard. He had only the most tenuous hold over the beast. She saw herself through the blazing eyes of the monster that stood over her, a weak pathetic thing who couldn't withstand the raw power of its savage canines. She saw in his steady gaze her very death and closed her eyes to await the pain of those teeth in her throat. Vard had been right all along, his gift would be the death of her. Her heart broke at the memory of the child he'd never know and the guilt he would carry for eternity.

But nothing happened. The weight on her chest vanished and Alecia squinted through one eye. It was too dark to see anything. She opened both eyes. Vard was a black shape several paces along the track, a splotch of dark hair, long limbs and white teeth that slowly resolved into a man – her man. She heaved a huge sigh of relief. It wasn't her time. She held her position until she was sure the transformation was complete, then slowly rose to her feet.

"I've scared you," he said, his voice full of disgust. "What did I do? Are you hurt?"

"Can't you remember?"

"We were running with arrows buzzing past our ears." He stared at her with odd intensity. "You must never trust the transformation, Alecia. I remember staring into your eyes and thinking… feeling… Just never trust me in that form."

Alecia gazed at his face; a wolfish look lingered in his eyes. She shivered. He didn't trust himself, perhaps would never trust, no matter how much he learned of his talent.

"We must check the horses. They were spooked by your. . . form." She turned and walked back up the track to the clearing, approaching Swift and stroking his quivering shoulder. Her horse was in better shape. The poor animal was too stupid and slow to know real danger when it presented itself.

"Thank the Goddess that Aloe lied about removing our horses," Alecia said, and then a thought occurred. "Or were they moved and you found them by scent?"

Vard crossed the clearing, a wary look in his eye. "This is where I left them." He studied her as she checked the girths and arrayed the weapons on the saddles. "What did I do that scared you?"

She averted her gaze. "Nothing, Vard. I wasn't scared, or no more than usual. Now hush and mount. We have a long way to travel and enemies behind us." So saying, she swung into the saddle. He stared for a while longer, a frown on his face, then followed her lead. They took another narrow track out of the clearing, traveling southeast.

CHAPTER 13

VARD awoke in the dim grayness just before dawn, his limbs and mind weary with a fatigue he rarely felt. His rest hadn't been sound, and echoes of his nightmares returned to haunt him. At least he thought they were nightmares. It was difficult to sort dreams from the recollections he retained from the transformation. A flash of a blonde woman beneath him, eyes closed, his paw on her chest, seared his mind. It felt real. Had he stood over Alecia like that, regarding her as prey, salivating at the thought of warm flesh in his stomach? Fear gripped his heart and he sat up. She had made her bed across the campfire. Even as he watched, she tossed and muttered in her sleep.

He sighed and leaned back against a rock. Alecia had been withdrawn since the end of their flight from the *Sis Lenweri*. Something had changed for her, and despite what she said, she had been afraid. *Of me.* Had she finally seen she was in real danger if she stayed? Would he wake one morning to find her gone and spend the rest of his days wondering if she was dead or alive? Not long ago he would have said Alecia would only leave him when the sun stopped rising, but after the last two months he wasn't so sure. She had retreated from him.

He rose and placed more wood on the fire, before fetching water from the nearby stream for porridge and tea. As he placed the pot on the fire, Alecia stirred.

"Good morning," she said, pushing herself upright.

The fastenings of her tunic had unraveled during the night and Vard caught a flash of white breast that peeked through the sagging fabric. His loins tightened in desire and he dragged his gaze to her face. The look of fear was still there, but it did little to quell the desire he felt, heightened as it was by weeks of deprivation. He crossed to her and knelt, one hand reaching for her face. Despite the fear in her gaze, she turned her cheek into his palm and kissed the calluses there.

Hot desire flooded him and he looped his other arm around her to draw her body to his. He must feel those lips on his skin, must feel alive as only Alecia made him feel. He could control the transformation; he must, because he could no longer keep her at arm's length.

She stiffened in his arms, but his lips claimed hers, forcing them apart and thrusting his tongue to explore the soft warm spaces in her mouth. His hand dropped to her breast, frustrated with the tunic that barred his touch. The fastenings came loose, and she moaned as his fingers caressed hard nipples, her hips arching toward his. Goddess, she was so beautiful, lush and ripe and ready. And he needed her as he never had before. The weeks of deprivation and frustration surged up to overwhelm him and he laid her back and tore the remaining tunic from her body, pulled the breeches from her hips, and stroked the wetness between her legs. She moaned again and arched her hips, as eager as he for the coupling.

As Vard stood and removed his breeches, swearing at the buttons that would not obey his fingers, a picture flashed into his head of two wolves mating, and he froze. That hadn't happened before. What did it mean? But Alecia chose that moment to moan and arch her hips again and he fell upon her, forcing her legs wider and plunging his sex into her, lost in the rhythm of life, reducing the act of love to one of basic animal instinct. He bent to suck her nipples, one after the other, thrusting into her after he tasted each breast and repeating the process over and over. Alecia must have felt the raw animal lust too, because she thrust up at him just as hard and screamed his name the moment his seed burst within her. He collapsed onto her body, the sweat of their exertion mixing with the molten heat of their union.

Despite the base nature of their coupling, Vard felt a deep closeness with Alecia, not wanting to sever the attachment in that moment for fear they would never again recapture it. He stayed inside her and shifted a little so he could observe her. She looked up at him, the shadow of fear in her eyes as it often had been lately.

"What's the matter?" he said.

She frowned. "You took me like an animal. I don't know if I liked it."

Vard laughed. "Oh, you liked it. Your reactions were very much unlike the princess you are, but that's acceptable when you couple with your mate."

"We did it like animals, Vard. I feel dirty."

"Are you saying you didn't wish for sex?"

Alecia hesitated. "No, I… I'm not sure what I wanted, only that you initiated it and I was swept up in the act."

"You screamed my name as you climaxed. I felt you tighten around me. Don't tell me you took no pleasure."

Now Vard was angry. He felt his sex swell where it lay within her and her eyes opened wide as she felt it too. He rose over her again and his head dipped, his teeth grasping her neck below her left ear. He thrust deeper into her. Alecia groaned, arching her head back to expose her neck and his teeth gripped her skin tighter as he thrust again.

Her body stiffened and she cried out. "You're hurting me, Vard. Please, stop."

He froze, looking down upon her as she lay naked and shivering, her blonde hair a tangled mess, the musky scent of their coupling swirling between them. The animal within him wanted to ignore her plea but the pain and fear in her lilac eyes forced him away. He rolled off her and stood, looking down at her.

"What just happened, Alecia?"

"You were hurting me." She stood up and gathered her clothes, holding them before her like a shield. "I'm going to wash," she said, putting snow into a pan and pouring boiling water over it. "I'd appreciate some privacy."

Vard stared at her bare back for a long moment, questions arising but none he was willing to voice. She needed space so he'd give it to her. Alecia had a quick temper, but she always saw reason in the end.

This time would be no different. He stalked from the clearing, already forming the hawk in his mind. A juicy rabbit for breakfast would make her feel better; food in the stomach always did.

* * *

Alecia followed Vard through the forest on her old nag and for once the forbidding environment was the last thing on her mind. She had washed and they'd breakfasted, before pushing on through the forest. The meal had been tense, with no words spoken unless needed. She was sick with fear. Vard had frightened her, again. Yes, he had stopped when she asked him, so there had been no forcing of the sexual act upon her, but what had come over him this morning? He had always been tender. Passionate, yes, but not rough. He had been like an animal, like the wolf of yesterday.

She closed her eyes and breathed deeply, trying to calm her racing heart, but memories flashed into her mind of Vard looming over her, nipping and sucking her breasts and thrusting into her until he climaxed, almost snarling her name. Where was the tender Vard who had taught her about love? Had he somehow slipped further from control during his time with Leth? Might there come a time when he couldn't stop? When she would be completely at his mercy? She shook her head, the questions making her skull ache.

* * *

Vard sat stiff in the saddle, his mind far away. Even so, a part of him observed the forest through which they rode. It was unchanged from their last visit, the trees bunched close, and mist and fog hugging the canopy, tendrils drifting down toward the travelers. They each rode wrapped in their own world, Vard dreading the time when they would stop, and he must face her.

Alecia acted almost as though he had raped her, when he knew… he *knew…* she had wanted their coupling as much as he. All those weeks of denial, the frustration building day by day, had resulted in neither of them having proper control over their actions. But he had stopped when asked, so why did she treat him like the enemy now? Perhaps he had been caught up in the animal act, but he was sure Alecia had no reason to hate him. His free hand punched his thigh in anger. All he wished for was to protect her, and if he had hurt her in this way...

The hairs on the back of his neck stirred and he had the feeling of being watched. He stopped Swift and dismounted, handing the reins to Alecia.

"Stay here with the horses. I'm going to scout our back trail."

"Why?"

"I want to lay a false track to discourage pursuit."

Alarm flared in her eyes. "You think the *Sis Lenweri* still chase us?"

"I don't know but it would be wise to assume so. I don't want you to worry. All will be well."

She shook her head. "I don't think it will."

Vard gazed up at her beautiful lilac eyes and feared he'd never again see love shining from them. *Better that than dead lilac eyes*. He resisted the urge to stroke her hand. "I won't be away long." He turned and stalked back up the track.

Vard back-tracked to a small stream, removing the evidence of their passing as he went. He waded up the watercourse to strike a false trail further into the bush, then transformed into the hawk and flew back to Alecia. Her eyes were upon him as he regained human form. He dropped from the low branch, running his fingers through his hair to straighten the wind-tousled strands, and walked to his horse. "No sign of pursuit and I've laid another trail. I'll continue to do so until we reach safety." He didn't mention his concern that, were Leth following, very little would stop the sorcerer from finding them.

"I'll never grow accustomed to your animal forms," she said, a frown on her brow and her eyes clouded with doubt.

He shrugged and climbed upon his horse, pulling his reins from her fingers as he did so. "Let's gallop for a while and we may clear this forest before dark." He spurred Swift forward, flicking a glance back to ensure Alecia followed.

* * *

They broke through the trees on the fringe of the forest at dusk that day. Alecia gazed up at the deep gray clouds clinging to the mountains before her and shivered. There would be snowfall that night, unless she was mistaken. Dark and foreboding though the forest might have been, it provided a degree of protection against the elements, and at this moment anything was preferable to facing a blizzard. She glanced at Vard. He caught her eye and frowned but she clucked to her horse and pushed on into the stony foothills of the Usetar Mountains.

A blizzard did indeed strike that night but Vard managed to find a shallow cave on the leeward side of the storm. They huddled together for warmth in front of a pitiful excuse for a fire. Alecia sat, wrapped in misery, heartsick that she should again feel the fear of Vard's true self. Yes, she had succumbed to it when she first uncovered his secret but had thought herself long past those feelings. Now she wondered how she had ever believed it could be right between them, that they might have a future? She had been naïve, so much in love, that she hadn't allowed herself to admit to the danger. But now it wasn't only her life but her child's. So far, she had escaped harm but now it seemed there must come a day when her luck, and Vard's tenuous control, would fail.

Soon after dinner, Vard suggested they retire for the night. At least in sleep Alecia hoped she could escape the gut-wrenching tension that cloaked her companionship with him. She was mistaken. Dreams plagued her and she relived the primitive intercourse that Vard had inflicted upon her, but magnified in its violence and lust.

She awoke before dawn, a scream on her lips that echoed within the cave and radiated out over the white landscape. A calloused hand clamped over her mouth and she struggled against the pressure, her heart raging in her chest like a savage animal's. Fury swept over her as she realized it was Vard.

"Get your hands off me!"

He recoiled as if stung. "It was the only way I could think to keep you quiet."

She wiped her lips with the back of her hand, swallowing the terror that still threatened to undo her. Eyes darting around the shallow cave and across the snow-covered hills, she desperately tried to bring herself back to reality, back to the nightmare of yesterday.

Vard's eyes still dwelt upon her. "You don't have to be this way," he said, quietly. "We must work together if we're to reach safety."

"You should have thought of that before you…" Her voice ended on a sob.

"I didn't mean to frighten you, Alecia. You must believe me. I can't live my life knowing you think I hurt you intentionally."

"Then you admit hurting me?"

"I stopped when you asked me. We were both caught up in the moment. You know I desire you, more than anyone I've ever had in my life. All the weeks of frustration. . ."

Her chin came up. "Excuses."

"I've said sorry." He stood and began scraping snow into a pot. "I'll start breakfast."

She watched as he prepared the meal, the stubborn set to his mouth signaling eloquently that the matter was far from a resolution.

The next week or so brought more of the same – Vard stubbornly defending his actions, insisting he was sorry, and Alecia cold and fearful of the future. It made her sad to her very core and she rode, her arm cradled across her stomach, as if to console the child within.

The week passed with Alecia knowing few blessings other than the shelter of a cave over her head most nights. She knew Vard transformed into the wolf to find these shelters, even though he tried to hide the fact from her. He had a certain look after the transformation, his eyes golden, wild and not quite human.

The one night they didn't look for a cave was their stop at the Barans. The farm was deserted, the animals gone, and the doors closed against the winter. Alecia took comfort in seeing the farmhouse and outbuildings secured, as this wouldn't have been the case if the Barans had been driven out or ambushed.

"Perhaps they moved to Brightcastle," she said, as they roamed through the farmhouse, looking for food. There was little left, another reason for optimism. Their departure had been planned.

Vard said nothing but set about building a fire with the dry wood stored in the woodshed. Once the fire was laid, Alecia prepared a meal of rabbit stew with the last of their provisions. Tomorrow they would go hungry unless Vard caught more game. After the meal, she sat back in Mistress Baran's rocking chair, staring at the fire and dreaming of how her babe would look. Would the child be a son with dark hair and sea green eyes, or a daughter with blonde hair and a startled lilac gaze?

* * *

Vard sat on the floor with his back to the wall, slightly to the rear of Alecia so he could observe her without her noticing. She was so beautiful, desirable no matter what she wore. Her long legs stretched toward the fire drew his attention to what rested between them, out of sight but very much in his mind. The ripe mounds of her breasts heated his loins as they rose and fell with her breathing. And the way the firelight played across her face softened the hard light that had entered her violet orbs this last week. His loins ached to have her, to make her his again, to mate and satiate the need that rose within.

He gritted his teeth and looked away, desperate to bring his feelings back under control. He couldn't risk scaring her again. Already too much harm had been caused by a few unguarded moments. But she didn't hate him, not yet. He still saw love in that gaze when she thought he wasn't looking, still saw wistfulness, and that could only mean he had another chance to mend their love. But as much as he wished to restore their relationship, he didn't know if he dared. His control rode a knife edge, wavering between man and beast, especially when it came to his feelings for Alecia. Might it not be best to leave her while there was this rift between them? At least now she wouldn't fight his departure.

He shook his head in denial as he had a hundred times since stepping beyond the bounds of human love into animal lust. What was happening to him? Alecia was the one good thing in his life, and he'd found a way to hurt her. Without speaking, he reached for his blanket, wrapped himself in it and turned his back on temptation.

* * *

It was the coldest day yet and they had no food left. Alecia's stomach growled as she loaded her bow on the saddle and tied her saddlebags in place. She walked back to the door of the farmhouse and closed it, then mounted and rode out of the farmyard with Vard. They took a broad trail through open woodland, and the wind sliced across their path and cut through their cloaks. Alecia rode with a sense of deep foreboding. They were only a day away from the Andra's farm and there was every chance that Vard would leave her there. What would she do if he abandoned her? Equally, this wary companionship their relationship had sunk to couldn't last. She didn't want to say goodbye and yet she hated the anxiety that filled her at the thought he might hurt her and her child. Alecia couldn't regain the optimism she had always felt; that their love could conquer anything.

She watched his back as he rode ahead of her, just far enough that conversation was impossible but not so far that he couldn't respond if there were trouble. Broad shoulders were accentuated by the gray cloak he wore, and everything about his posture spoke of confidence and capability. Well, almost everything. Alecia thought she could detect just a slight hunch to those shoulders, as if he were aware of the thoughts of the woman behind him and knew they accused him.

Alecia swallowed to release the lump in her throat. She was as afraid to be with Vard as she was petrified to leave him. He wouldn't admit his wrongdoing and she wasn't even certain it had been wrong. Her lack of experience wouldn't let her decide, but, before Amitania, her life with Vard had shown her nothing of the man who frightened her with his violent love-making. Could she blame Leth's influence? Was this part of some elaborate plan to separate them so he could use her for his own schemes? Divide and conquer?

A fluttering in her abdomen disturbed her thoughts and it took a moment for Alecia to realize the sensation was the movement of her babe in its warm cocoon. She laid her hand protectively over her stomach, but the contact with her babe brought her sadness instead of joy. She imagined herself cast adrift in a hostile world with a child. Perhaps her father would take her back, even though she'd obviously be soiled goods.

He could pass the child off as that of a mistress, and Alecia would be protected from the wagging tongues of the kingdom. He might even name her child his heir if it were a boy. Her gut twisted at the thought, the feeling so wrong she knew, even before her babe was born, she could never disown him.

They traveled thus for most of the day, speaking only when needed, each locked in a cold and silent world of their own. There was no sign of any other travelers, but the small prints of hares abounded in the area. As night began to close in, Vard found another shallow cave and Alecia set up their campsite while he stalked into the forest. She frowned as she watched him leave and then turned to prepare the fire for the fresh meat he'd bring back.

As she toiled, she had the feeling of eyes upon her but could discern nothing when she scanned the forest. Through the sparse trees, she could see for a hundred yards in every direction. An animal squealed and the sound was cut short, the hairs on the back of her neck rising. When she turned from the fire again, the wolf stood gazing at her, golden eyes aglow, two freshly dead hares dangling from his jaws.

She gasped and fell on her backside, eyes riveted to the huge black creature. Thick red blood dripped to the snow beneath his jaws, but all Alecia could contemplate were those teeth in her throat, should he swap rabbit for princess.

"Please, Vard," she said, scrabbling backward in the snow past the fire pit. He watched her and took a step forward, a low growl rumbling in his neck.

"Oh, Goddess protect me." Her voice scraped past a throat tight with terror.

The wolf took another pace toward the fire pit and dropped the hares, his eyes never leaving her face. His lip curled again showing sharp canines and he seemed to lean backward, tensed as if to spring for her throat. She wanted to close her eyes to block the dreadful picture but was transfixed by the terrible promise in Vard's feral gaze.

She thought of her child whose life would be lost along with hers. "Please Vard, it's me, Alecia." What could she say to him to trigger the human within the wolf? Her frantic mind searched for and discarded people from Vard's past both recent and long ago: Leth, his cousin Frel, her father, Lord Finus – she shivered at the thought of the last even through her terror of Vard. She was loath to mention any name that might trigger an attack rather than bring Vard back to her. Finally, she realized her mistake.

Prey. She was behaving like prey: cowering, prone, her soft belly exposed. Perhaps if she convinced Vard she wasn't vulnerable, he would back off. She levered herself slowly up into a seated position and the wolf backed up a step. Moving inch by inch, muscle by muscle, she rose to a crouch, then slowly to stand, never taking her eyes from the beast. He backed up further, stopped snarling, and stood gazing at her. What next? It was still an impasse, but Alecia felt she had strengthened her position. Now to get Vard back. It was a risk, but she took a step toward him, her heart threatening to pound its way out of her chest. She desperately hoped he couldn't hear it, or he'd know she was still prey.

If a wolf could be said to frown, he frowned. His eyebrows twitched and the fire went out of his eyes. He sat in the snow and a shimmering began around his form. The wolf became a misty thing and then Vard sat there, head in hands, his shoulders trembling. She reached out to him before she could think and, taking a few steps forward, laid her hand on his shoulder. He stiffened and looked up at her, eyes wet with tears.

"You're the bravest woman in the world," he said. "I was a heartbeat from leaping onto you and ripping your throat out, and you stood and took a step toward me. How did you know exactly the right thing to do?"

Alecia gasped. "How did you remember that? You can't recall things so well usually."

"I don't know, but it was as if I was trapped in the wolf's mind. I could see with my eyes but had no control over the creature. It hasn't happened before. Had you said or done anything else, you would have died…" His voice broke and tears slid down cheeks roughened by stubble. "I couldn't bear to watch helpless as I killed you…" He raised his eyes to hers and despair shone from them. "Take that bow and shoot me. I won't stop you."

"No!"

"Don't you see, Alecia? I was very nearly the cause of your death! Do us both a favor. I grow tired of the fight."

Indeed, his eyes carried the weight of years of battling his true nature and losing, the burden of death on his conscience, and no prospect of gaining control of his gift. How could he not despair?

"You're right to hate me," he said.

Alecia looked at him for a long time, trying to puzzle out how she felt. "I don't hate you. You're a victim. We both are. But that doesn't change anything. You allowed your animal drives to violate the trust I had in you. And just now I thought I was dead."

"I've told you all along you risked your life with me," Vard said quietly. "I was weak to allow you to stay, weak to let you convince me there was hope for us; to think we could have some time together. I was wrong and I'm sorry."

Tears coursed down Alecia's cheeks. After weeks of denial she must accept the fact - she couldn't have Vard in her life. She wasn't blameless either. She hadn't told him of his child. Would that knowledge have made a difference? Would awareness of her fragility have stayed his hand that morning? Should she tell him now? She had all but made the decision to leave him; should she now tell him he was to be a father? *No!* Not yet. She still had time before Vard walked out of her life. Alecia's heart ached at the mere thought of him leaving without her, but he'd been right all along. Until Vard mastered control of his transformations, she had to stay away from him, perhaps forever.

"See me to the Andra's and you can continue your search for a mentor," she said, her voice breaking with the strain of holding back her tears. Anger drove more tears into her eyes; anger at herself for being weak over a man. She didn't even recognize the girl who had roamed Brightcastle rescuing witches and killing mercenaries. It seemed like another life; one she'd have back if she could return to the relative innocence of life before Vard.

He echoed her thoughts. "You'll be all right, Alecia. You're a strong woman and you'll find a way to reclaim your life, to do the work you were born for. Take some time with the Andras to recover, then send word to Ramón. He'll come to fetch you." The words left a bitter twist to Vard's mouth.

He picked up the hares and began to skin them. All of a sudden, Alecia's appetite evaporated. Perhaps Ramón would welcome her back, perhaps even her father, but she couldn't return if Finus lived. She prayed every night he had succumbed to the sword thrust Vard dealt him. Regardless, Alecia vowed she'd never again place her destiny in her father's hands. *Never again.*

CHAPTER 14

A FTER a silent evening meal and a night of little sleep, Vard and Alecia set out again and were within sight of the Andra farm by midmorning. Vard felt glad to have people around again after the strain of dealing with Alecia. He could hardly believe the depths to which their relationship had sunk, and it was all his doing. One of them had to take responsibility for what had happened, and he was the worldly soldier who should have realized the fragility of his sheltered princess.

He sighed deeply as he watched her ride just ahead of him.

After all her traumas, her spine was still straight and her head held high, every inch royalty. She'd need all that grit and determination to survive the ordeal ahead, for she'd have to return to Brightcastle eventually. His heart ached that he wouldn't be around to help her, but he had helped Alecia into this situation. His continued presence would only make her life more difficult.

A dog barked as they came up the road toward the farm. Master Andra appeared from the barn and the mistress from the house. They stood for a moment, then approached the front gate from their respective positions, casting glances at each other.

Mistress Andra reached the gate first as they dismounted.

"Welcome back, Princess," she said and dropped into a deep curtsy. She turned to Vard. "Captain." Her voice became guarded as though she caught some hint of the trouble between them. "It has been long since you passed, two months or more. Did you find what you sought?"

Vard nodded to Master Andra as he limped up. "We found what we sought but I fear it will be the cause of trouble. Why are you limping, Master Andra?"

The farmer rubbed his left thigh and grimaced. "An arrow from a blasted dark elf, Captain. I was hunting just north of here and felt a pain in my leg. Another dart flew straight after the first, then more still as I walloped my horse out of there. I know the arrows of dark elves when I see them, even if the flaming critters didn't show themselves. Blasted black mongrels."

"Thom! The princess!" Mistress Andra said, turning to Alecia. "You look tired, Princess."

"Nothing that a good night's sleep won't help, Mistress," Alecia said.

Vard looked sharply at Alecia and noted for the first time the deep shadows beneath her eyes. How could he have been so caught up in his own misery that the condition of his lady went ignored? Well, soon her care wouldn't be his responsibility. He felt a pang of regret for a life he would never know. But she'd be better off eventually. Better that than dead. Already she carried emotional scars that would be with her forever.

Mistress Andra looked from Vard to Alecia and back again. She opened her mouth and he braced himself for more questions but Master Andra forestalled her.

"Come, mother, we mustn't keep Princess Alecia and Captain Anton at the gate. I'll take the horses and you show them to the fire."

While Vard removed their weapons and saddlebags, Alecia stood staring at the snow until Mistress Andra took her by the hand and led her over to the house. Once he had hung their possessions on hooks in the front entry, Vard found Alecia ensconced in the rocking chair in front of the fire.

Mistress Andra drew Vard into the kitchen, a deep frown on her broad forehead. "What is amiss, Captain? The princess is much changed since last I saw her."

He grimaced. "There have been. . . difficulties, but she is well, I think."

"I don't think she's well at all, Captain, but if you don't wish to discuss the matter, I'll respect that for now."

Vard grimaced again as the woman crossed to the pot that bubbled over the fire. She had discerned the trouble between him and Alecia with only the briefest of examinations and, knowing women, blamed him; a very astute woman indeed. He decided to check on the horses.

* * *

Alecia gazed at the flickering flames of the fire, her thoughts not on anything in particular. It was a luxury to be warm and unafraid again. It seemed months since she had felt that way. It *had* been months. She rested her hands over her abdomen, feeling again the butterfly wings of her babe's movement in her womb. Mistress Andra brought her a mug of sweetened tea.

"Lunch will be ready soon, Princess, but I thought you could use a hot drink." Her eyes fell to Alecia's abdomen and her voice lowered even though the room was empty. "You are with child?"

She jerked her head up. She'd have to confide in the woman if she was to stay for any length of time. There was no point delaying the moment. "I am."

"The captain doesn't know?"

Alecia shook her head, eyes low.

"The babe is his?"

That made her head snap up again, a wave of indignity crashing over her. "Of course! What do you take me for?"

Mistress Andra frowned as if a puzzle lay before her. "Then what is this trouble between you?"

Alecia gaped. "There is no trouble between us."

Mistress Andra crouched beside her chair, taking her cold hands in rough warm ones. "You don't have to hide your pain from me, Princess. I see the distance between you and Captain Anton. If the babe is his, what's amiss?"

Alecia longed to tell the woman it was none of her business, but the motherly brown eyes froze her tongue. "I've not told him," she said, wringing her hands in her lap. "It sounds silly now I explain it. At first, I hesitated because I feared he'd leave me behind where he thought I'd be safe. I didn't want that, Mistress Andra. More recently there have been harsh words between us, trouble I don't think we will overcome."

Her voice had risen, and the motherly farmwife hushed her, rubbing her hands and then pushing the mug of tea at her. "I won't tell Captain Anton anything you don't wish me to."

Alecia bit her lip to stop it from trembling, to hold her composure together in the face of Mistress Andra's sympathy.

It was this picture Vard was greeted with, as he stepped back into the house amid a flurry of snow. He took one long look at them and the gold of his eyes flared in the dim light of the farmhouse. Before Alecia could think of anything to say, he turned and stalked back out, slamming the door.

"He has a temper that one, if you don't mind me saying so, Princess. I begin to see the problems you face."

"You can't begin to imagine until you walk in our shoes," she said, her heart miserable. "I hope one day I may be able to explain all to you, but for now you'll have to be patient."

Mistress Andra smiled and patted Alecia on the head, which only served to make her grind her teeth.

"I'm sure we all imagine we suffer more than others, Princess, but when all's said and done, it's only exchanging one difficulty for another. When you look back in a few months, you'll laugh at what you cried over today."

Alecia sighed heavily but held her tongue and nodded. Three months on the road with Vard had given her independence that didn't sit well in Mistress Andra's presence.

* * *

Vard was doing some teeth grinding of his own. Chips of wood flew from the blade of the axe as he split one log after another. Already he had a moderate pile of firewood cut and he would cut all night if he had to. Better that than facing the accusing glances of the farm wife. One look into the farmhouse had been enough to sketch the details. Mistress Andra had looked at him as if he were a beast from the swamplands come to take her children, and Alecia had looked as guilty as hell. What had she told the woman?

He placed one more log on the stump and added to the pile with another savage blow. Had she revealed every sordid detail? A larger log and another crushing blow. It was none of the woman's concern. The snow whirled around but Vard didn't notice as his body moved with the rhythm of a woodsman. He needed something physical to vent his anger and frustration. That was the entirety of his existence the past two months, and before that if he were honest. Small wonder it had all come to a head with Alecia.

No excuses. He was a beast, and it was best he left her before he did something irrevocable.

The trouble was, just the scent of her drove him wild with desire. The way her hair lay across her cheek at night, the smile that lit her face in unexpected delight, her laughter at the oddest moments. All this he would never forget, and suspected he couldn't live long without. But it was no longer his decision. She didn't want him near her. Shame coursed through him and he came to a halt, resting the axe on the stump, split timber lying all around. His gasping breath shot great gouts of steam into the cold air. He spun around as a hand grasped his shoulder, his eyes coming to rest on the craggy face of Master Andra.

"Time to come in, Captain."

Vard stared at the man until his hand dropped.

"It's none of my business…"

"No, it's not, Master Andra, and I'd rather harsh words weren't said between us." Vard dropped the axe against the chopping stump. "I have a request to make of you."

The farmer hunched his shoulders and drew the collar of his coat around his ears but said nothing.

He's not going to help me out at all. "I desire to leave the princess with you when I go. How safe would she be here?"

Master Andra frowned. "If you mean how safe would she be from Prince Zialni and her betrothed, then I think not very safe."

"The prince has visited since we were last here?"

"No, Captain. I've had no more news of the prince or Lord Finus. My wound and the winter have kept me cabin bound, and even with the spring on its way I don't know how I'll plant the crops, let alone get them to market."

"I'm sorry to ask this of you, but I can't take her with me when I leave. Her safety would be at risk."

"My wife and I would do all in our power to protect the princess, even should the prince once again send his mercenaries, as he did when our son lost his life." He paused and Vard saw raw hurt in the old man's eyes. Life in old age would be hard for the Andras without their only son. "Is the princess ill?"

Vard shook his head. "No, just tired." *And heartsick, he added to himself.* His mood darkened even further at the thought of leaving her behind. "Nothing that a few days of rest and good food can't repair. I thank you in anticipation of your help."

Master Andra smiled. "It's a small sacrifice to help her. She's our princess, and she loved our son. Now, if I don't warm my old bones soon, I won't be alive to care for Princess Alecia." The old man stomped inside, followed by Vard, whose core had started to chill at the prospect of confronting Mistress Andra and Alecia together.

* * *

Alecia jumped, her heart threatening to hammer out of her chest as the knock came at her door. It was such an impatient sound, she knew immediately Vard was on the other side.

"Come." She drew the covers up over her chest, suddenly needing the heated brick that lay wrapped in a blanket beneath her toes. What could he have to say to her after the meal they had just shared? There were no words that could mend the rift between them or prepare her for his abandonment.

Alecia stifled a gasp as Vard slipped through the door and closed it behind him. He looked dreadful, dark circles under his striking green-gold eyes, his face haggard where before he had looked vital and fit. She mustn't feel sorry for him. It wouldn't do her any good. She probably looked no better.

Something weighed upon his soul and she presumed it must be their misfortune. Her heart cried out for the early days of their love when they had been sustained by mutual need. Clearly, Vard felt more than his fair share of hunger for her body but a relationship couldn't live on lust alone.

"Princess."

Despair tore through her at the formality of his words. Since when had she been "princess"? Her chin rose, and she imagined her lilac gaze cutting at his sorrow. "Yes?"

"I leave at first light in the morning. This is goodbye."

Her resolve wavered but she held firm. "I see." *Tell him!*

He took a step toward the bed and she steeled herself not to reach for him.

"I hate to leave things between us as they are," he said, "but I believe this to be the best course of action. Perhaps one day you'll forgive me, but if not, at least I'll know you're safe."

She thought of the babe within and couldn't imagine the months ahead, or the birth, without him. That would likely kill her. Would it change his decision if she told him of the child? "Where will you go?"

"I have some vague thought to head north and take the road east at the foot of the Usetar Mountains." His eyes flared golden in the candlelight and her breath caught at his magnificence. "I'll find my mentor, Alecia, but you must accept that I'll not be back. I'd never ask you to wait for me, even if I thought you wanted to."

As he stared at her, perhaps drinking in one last picture of the girl she knew he adored, she dropped her eyes lest he see the love she still had for him. He had made his decision and it was for the best. If she told him she was with child, it would only make him question whether he should leave. Best to have a clean break. She swallowed several times before she could trust her voice would be strong. "I wish you success in your search, Vard, and may the Goddess protect you until… May the Goddess protect you."

Vard strode around the bed and grasped her hand, bringing it to his mouth. His lips trembled against her skin and it was nearly the undoing of her. "Farewell, my love."

He was gone as quickly as he had entered her life in that lonely alley months before. Alecia thrust her face into her hands and wept.

CHAPTER 15

ALECIA slept late the next morning, having been awake and miserable most of the night. Vard had been a tangible presence on the other side of the door and she battled with herself all night; had to stop herself from going to him on occasions too numerous to recall. But she had held her nerve and now he'd be gone. She levered herself up out of bed and wrapped a heavy shawl around her shoulders. Head pounding, she stepped from the bedroom to find a cheerful blaze in the kitchen hearth and a bowl of oatmeal kept warm by a hot stone near the fire. Bright sunlight streamed through the windows, lifting the misery that had settled on Alecia's heart. But there was no sign of Vard.

Mistress Andra bustled in from the farmyard, a bowl of eggs in her hand.

"Good morning, Princess. I let you sleep as you were poorly yesterday. How do you feel?"

Alecia shrugged the question off. "Where is the captain?"

Mistress Andra frowned. "Gone. At first light. He said he had bid you farewell last night, so I didn't interfere."

Alecia nodded.

"Did I do right?"

"Yes, Mistress, you were correct not to wake me. The captain and I have said all that needs to be said." She ran her hands over her abdomen and Mistress Andra frowned again at the gesture.

"It's such a pity that the babe's father won't be here for his birth. He still has no knowledge?"

"No," Alecia said more sharply than she intended, "and it will stay that way. Yesterday's goodbye was once and forever."

"None of us know what's in the future, Princess, especially when we are joined by a child."

"I can't think about that." Alecia fetched the bowl of porridge and sat with it at the table, spooning generous quantities of honey onto the mixture.

Her companion stood with her arms folded. "You'll give birth to a healthy child and he'll make you proud. One day he'll know his father."

The hairs on the back of Alecia's neck stood on end and she looked at Mistress Andra. "That sounds like prophecy." There was no response. "Is it?"

She laughed off the question. "I'm no prophetess, Princess, just a friend who is trying to cheer you up."

Alecia smiled. "I don't suppose you can continue to call me 'princess' if I shall be with you for months. My name is Alecia."

"And mine is Dana."

She smiled and ate her porridge, doing her best to push thoughts of Vard from her mind.

* * *

Vard shuffled deeper into his cloak and thought fondly of the Andra's warm home, now several days ride to the south. Snow threatened again and Swift had been unsettled since he tethered him at dusk. The logs in the fire crackled but the snapping of the sap set his nerves on edge. He massaged the tight muscles across his shoulders and up his neck, but no amount of kneading seemed to smooth away his tension these days.

With nothing to restrain his transformation except the usual fear of being trapped, Vard had shifted into the wolf twice today, reveling in the freedom of movement through the snowy landscape and allowing his mind to truly embrace the predator. He had even enjoyed a brief run with a she-wolf until the creature had backed up to him. Spring was on its way but that was far more than Vard was willing to give. He shook his head as he imagined being the father of wolf cubs, if that was even possible. Damn, he should know all this, and still critical knowledge eluded him.

A strong eddy of wind tore through the small clearing bringing with it a flurry of snow. Vard looked up, sensing a threat. The wind grew until a great gale howled around him and he threw up his arms to ward off the stinging snow. The wind died and when he dropped his arms, Leth stood before him.

The sorcerer was dressed all in black – breeches, shirt and tunic – with silver embroidery on collar and cuffs and a sword at his hip. Vard had a fleeting thought that Leth had magically appeared but then saw the white horse behind him, all but disappearing into the wintery backdrop. He climbed to his feet, eyes never leaving Leth, thankful for the sword still buckled at his waist.

The silence stretched as Leth stared, a neutral expression on his face. His eyes told another story. The man was furious.

"You left without saying goodbye, Anton. Is that the way you repay someone who has tried to help you?"

"No, that's not the way I treat someone who has helped me." Vard tried to keep his own face as flat as Leth's but it was difficult as the anger built within. "However, all your training has brought me is frustration. I don't believe you've genuinely tried to teach me anything."

Leth's mask vanished, his brows dropping until they almost obliterated his eyes, his lip curling into a snarl. "Ingratitude! It's not my fault you're a dunce." His eyes flickered around the camp. "Where is the princess?"

"Somewhere you'll not trouble her, you mad bastard. I know you had plans for her. That's why we left."

Leth took a step forward, his eyes gleaming. "I did have plans for Princess Alecia and since you won't leave this clearing alive, I'll tell you of them." He drew his sword from the scabbard. "I'll find your delicious princess and make her mine. She'll not be able to resist my powers of… persuasion. We'll return to Brightcastle and dispose of her father and any others who stand in my way. Soon I'll be king of

Thorius and your princess will produce heirs to ensure the vitality of my line." He paused for effect. "Indeed, she may already be pregnant with my seed."

Shock hit Vard and his mind reeled, his breath hard to summon. He swayed before pulling himself upright. "You've touched her?"

"Oh, I have done a lot more than touch her Anton. I have lain with her, sampled her ripe womanhood. It is a pity you were there first, but virgins are overrated."

Fury swept through Vard, clear thought swept away by betrayal and anger and hurt. How could she do this to him? How could Alecia betray their relationship by sleeping with Leth? Was it compulsion? Perhaps she hadn't known what she was doing? *No!* He couldn't allow himself to believe she was blameless in this. Better to give her the full weight of responsibility. Had he left her pregnant with Leth's child?

Too late, he realized that Leth moved toward him, sword waving in the air between them. Vard drew his sword and stepped backward, desperately trying to bring his thoughts under control. He couldn't win this with anger. Leth didn't relent.

"Her breasts are my favorite feature, I think," he said, surging forward and bringing his sword in a sweeping arc toward Vard's skull. The blow was blocked in desperation, Vard scrabbling for calm amidst thoughts of Alecia's breasts bared for Leth's fingers. He leapt away, breathing deeply, thoughts still battering at his brain like moths in a jar.

"Just the thought of that white stomach, round and full with my seed, makes me hard," the vile enchanter said, then swept in, his sword angled upward. Vard felt the tip catch on the front of his tunic as he threw himself backward. Without lightening quick reflexes, his guts would now be poured out on the snow. But Leth didn't pause. His tongue reached for the next jibe.

"And the thought of her flesh, rich and ripe for the taking…"

Vard ducked under a wild swing of his opponent's sword and spun to get his balance, but before he could attack, Leth was ready again. The man was at least equally as proficient as Vard at swordplay but how could he talk and be so effective? Perhaps that was his tactic.

Talk any rubbish and get his opponent angry enough that they made a mistake. Vard quashed the thoughts that swirled through his mind. He knew beyond a doubt he couldn't fight well when angry, with his thoughts in turmoil. Somehow, he must quiet his mind, but how, when the sorcerer rabbited on about Alecia in the most disgusting way?

He grasped the amber talisman at his throat, pouring his thoughts into it, storing all the anger and frustration of the last few months within the tawny stone. Slowly his calm returned, but not quickly enough to prevent Leth scoring a deep cut across his upper arm. His fingers on the sword loosened and the weapon almost slipped from his grasp. Leth saw the momentary weakness and pressed his attack, Vard backing off under the onslaught of dozens of lightening slashes, just barely managing to block several killing blows. He had to end this soon or he'd lose too much blood. He couldn't leave Alecia vulnerable to Leth, no matter how she had betrayed him. His strength wavered at the thought. No matter what they had endured this last week or so, she had always been the epitome of all that was good and right in the world. And she had deceived him.

But if Leth walked from this clearing, he'd find Alecia in a matter of days and she'd become a pawn in his games. Vard couldn't allow that, even if it meant his death. As blood trickled down his arm and dripped from his elbow, his strength waned, and Leth's features blurred. This was what it came down to then – a sacrifice, his life for Alecia's. Perhaps then he'd receive absolution for Frel's death. He swallowed down the regret that burned its way into his throat and, gritting his teeth, welcomed the blade that pierced his skin as he slid his own blade up to the hilt through Leth's heart.

Vard awoke hours later, hot breath on his face and a heavy weight over his legs. For a moment he couldn't remember where he was, but the smell of blood and the searing pain in his left side came crashing in upon his awareness. Leth! His night vision allowed him to see the body of the sorcerer, stiff in death, slumped across his lower legs. As he sat up, waves of dizziness and pain were almost his undoing. Leth's sword was still buried in his side. Every breath drove a fire of agony into his gut, but he managed to seize the sword and pull it out. His cry of torment echoed around the clearing, causing Leth's white charger to snort dirt and snot over his shoulder.

"Thanks, boy," Vard said, trying to distract himself from the pain. Blood oozed from the wound edges and he packed the area with snow then lay back. Breath still brought pain but not the core-wrenching agony of before. When he was sure the bleeding had stopped, Vard rolled Leth's body off his legs and slid his sword free. Congealed blood marred the blade. He ran it over the snow and wiped it on Leth's tunic. It could wait for proper cleaning.

He sat there, looking at the sorcerer's dead face, beard and moustache frozen solid. Was he alone? It seemed unlikely but if not, where were his cronies? Did he think himself so far above Vard that he had not perceived him as a threat? None of this made any sense. For now survival was the goal. He'd been given a second chance at life and must grab it. If he made it past the next few days, perhaps he'd find his mentor and his place in the world.

Right now, he needed warmth. He clamped his teeth shut as they began to chatter. The fire had gone out and any dry wood was too far to reach in his condition. He looked around for Swift and found him only a few paces away. Praying this wouldn't be one of the times the beast allowed his fear to run free, he crawled through the snow, stopping to take several breathers along the way. Swift snorted as Vard reached him but didn't pull back as he caught at the stirrup leather and pulled himself to his feet. He hauled himself into the saddle and sagged forward over the cantle, his cheek brushing Swift's snow-covered mane.

* * *

Alecia woke with a start, sweat sliding between her breasts. She shivered as the cold air of the bedroom struck her chest, and hauled the blankets back over her nakedness. She lay curled on her side, one arm cradling her stomach.

"Don't worry, little one," she said to her unborn babe. "Papa is well. It was just a dream. Her heartbeat sounded loud in her ears and her breath came in great gasps that she was sure would be heard by the other occupants of the small farmhouse.

She so wished she didn't have such vivid dreams. Worry for Vard had constantly plagued her over the past three days since he had left, but when these nightmares disturbed her sleep, showing him afflicted with terrible injuries, she didn't know what to think or how to deal with them. Dana knew of them and said they were just the product of an overactive imagination and worry, but Alecia thought differently. She had experienced true dreams before and these felt the same. Vard might be hurt and out there somewhere in the snow. If she was right, he had fought Leth. Her nails pressed into her palms in frustration. The sorcerer could be on his way to the farm this very moment and what could she do about it? He would use her just as Vard had warned, and all their strife and sacrifice would be for nothing.

No! She wouldn't play the victim! She rose from the bed, drawing a blanket around her as she did so, and walked to the corner of the room. She lifted her bow and ran her hand down its smooth length then lay it down and gathered her knives and whet stone. Leth wouldn't find her unprepared. If he dared pursue her then he should beware. She ran the first knife over the stone, seeking the calm she had always found in sharpening her weapons. It eluded her. Instead, with each scrape of the metal over stone, Alecia found a new reason to despair.

How would she endure the weeks and months ahead without Vard? It had been so easy to be angry with him with his solid presence at her side, but now her overwhelming feeling was loneliness. She had taken to sleeping naked, running her fingers over her body, exploring all the places Vard had awoken and imagining they were his hands instead of hers. It helped her feel less alone for a few short moments, but she knew if she didn't break the habit, she'd go mad.

She dropped the knife and instead turned her thoughts to the tiny life within her womb. He was what was important now. Not Vard, not her, except as a vessel to carry this life they had created. The life of the child must be nurtured, and she would use that life to stay strong. But how she missed Vard's arms around her, his lips on hers, her name whispered against her hair. Cold winter settled in her heart.

* * *

Vard awoke, the shallow cave cold and bare coals in the fire pit. Everything ached as he pushed himself to the back of the grotto to collect more wood, but the wounds in his left arm and side radiated pulsating waves of agony. He knew it indicated infection and that it would be the end of him. Days he had lain in this cave, fighting the transformation and trying to stay warm, but now it came down to survival. He needed the resilience of the creatures of the wild, or today would be his last day on earth. Already, it might be too late.

The decision taken, he acted lest he change his mind. Grasping the amber talisman at his throat, he focused on the stone and formed the image of the wolf in his mind. Transformation brought its own vitality, the snap of energy radiating through his damaged arm and down to the wound in his side.

As the wolf, Vard felt more life and less harm. He flexed his left foreleg and found the limb able to bear his weight. His long red tongue lolled from his mouth in the canine equivalent of a grin. The wound in his side was somewhat more of a concern, and already fresh blood congealed on his fur. He gave the area a lick but whimpered at the gentle touch of his tongue. Fresh warm blood was what he needed, the power of the forest in a form that would restore his broken body. He limped from the cave, his huge paws leaving marks in the hard, dry snow.

Vard awoke in the cave, human once again and his horse disappeared. He hoped Swift had fled and not fallen victim to his ravenous drive for blood. He remembered reveling in the feel of soft, warm flesh against his fangs, felt again the power of fresh meat. Days spent as the wolf had cured his wounds almost completely, but he felt less human. It had been too long, but he had needed that time to heal. Something had changed in his head, and he sensed the wildness of the wolf lurked just below the surface, ready to obliterate his humanity.

The past weeks seemed a distant thing and he tried to focus on Alecia. But thought skittered away from human pursuits toward the hunt, paws pounding through snow in search of prey and a mate. Now was the season to find a she-wolf. . . *No!* There lay ruin. He had resisted the transformation to prevent this very thing. What good was he if he became the wolf, or worse – some half-wolf and half-human beast, trapped in a limbo between two existences?

It was a very real threat. He felt halfway there already. Vard rose and packed what little he still possessed and left the cave, heading east.

* * *

Alecia sat in the rocking chair and gazed at the flames in the fireplace. Dana hummed to herself over the bread-making, and Master Andra mended a harness on the window seat on the other side of the room. Alecia's dreams had stopped over the last few days, but then had returned this morning. The relief when the nightmares eased was a palpable thing, only slightly marred by her wondering what Vard was up to.

Her dreams this morning were of Vard in a shallow cave, looking more haggard than she had ever seen him. Dark growth covered his cheeks and his hair lay matted on his shoulders. His clothes were torn in places and blood stained his tunic. Golden eyes stared into the fire. He looked more the wolf than ever.

Sharp fingers of fear plucked at her heart, but she fought down dread and made herself examine the facts. If her dreams were true, then Vard was still alive and in his human form. His eyes …she shuddered at the feral light they contained…had been clear and free of fever. Vard might have survived whatever wounds he had received. But would he survive the next transformation? She simply must believe he was well and would continue to prosper.

The butterfly flutters in her abdomen told her that her babe was awake and hungry and so she pushed herself up out of her chair and walked into the kitchen.

CHAPTER 16

MONTHS passed, winter merging into spring, and then spring into summer. Alecia fell easily into the rhythm of the seasons on the farm. She didn't think she could have been so content without the child in her belly. Dana had said as much, speaking of her own pregnancies as a relaxed time of waiting. Perhaps the soothing presence of the farmwife played more than a little part as well.

Alecia could almost have declared herself happy. Her belly had swelled to alarming proportions and she wondered how something so large could ever escape via the passage that nature had fashioned. Dana assured her again that all would be well, but lately she had detected worry in the woman's eyes when they discussed the impending birth. Dana hadn't revealed the source of her fears and Alecia hadn't the courage to question too hard. She would deal with the pain and difficulty when her labor began. And she would deal with whatever feelings the babe engendered in her.

Dreams of Vard had been few and far between. When they came, Alecia couldn't make sense of them. She remembered little the following morning, only flashes of Vard's hairy face and ever grubbier clothing. When she glimpsed his eyes, they were more wolf than man. It was the eyes that made her wake screaming. She no longer knew what the dreams meant, but the day after was always difficult, her mood low, her back aching and her appetite absent.

Her days were now occupied with the small tasks of a farmwife, those she could still manage. Food had to be prepared, floors cleaned, clothes and sheets washed, and gardens weeded. Alecia was entranced by the mundane tasks that had never been her province, even considering her tendency to independence. In her previous world, that of a sheltered princess, independence had meant dressing herself and doing her own hair rather than having a maid do it for her. Now she was fully acquainted with the life of the ordinary woman and she found her chores curiously relaxing. She had never before been so aware of the turning of the seasons and their intimate connection to the chores on the farm. Life was uncomplicated and she wished that she could truly allow her roots to take hold in the land owned by the Andras.

She couldn't, of course. This brief sojourn would come to an end when her babe was born, and she was no closer to knowing what she'd do when she must move on. She truly had nowhere to turn, and so she avoided thinking about the next step her life would take after the birth.

On a balmy summer's day, Alecia had decided to weed the vegetable garden. It was quite amazing how the determined weeds had poked their heads above the soil at the first sprinkle of rain. They must be pulled lest they take the goodness from the soil. Fresh vegetables and herbs were all that stood in the way of illness out in these remote holdings. Dana Andra had a good stash of dried herbs from last summer, but they would need replenishing before long. Already Alecia had learned much from the farmwife, whose stoic acceptance of good and ill filled her with admiration.

As she pulled the weeds she marveled at the warm earth under her nails. The rich odor of the soil filled her nostrils, imbibing her with a heady delight that no fancy perfume had ever achieved. Only one scent had ever competed, and that was the musky scent of her captain. As if her thoughts had awoken the babe, her stomach heaved, the infant restless within her womb. She laid her hands over her abdomen, delighting in the movement within, as if a snake were writhing and twisting inside her.

"Soon, my love," she said, "soon we'll welcome you into the world." Sadness tainted her joy as she remembered there would only be one parent to welcome the child.

* * *

Ramón Zorba, Guardian of Brightcastle, rode Raven, his black mare, along the northern track ahead of half a dozen soldiers. He had chosen them himself and felt confident they were equal to the task they had been set. He smiled as he remembered their passage out of Brightcastle, the hopes of a kingdom resting on seven shoulders. Perhaps they would succeed where others had failed.

He shook thick blond hair from his eyes in order to see further ahead, adjusting the fur-lined blue cloak that rested on his shoulders and lay over his horse's rump. There was smoke up ahead, the spidery chimney smoke of a homestead. He frowned. Farmers out here were braver than he to run their holdings miles from civilization, at the mercy of bandits and the dark elves.

He only hoped Captain Vorasava was equal to the task of defending Brightcastle and his wife, Benae, during his short absence. But this was a mission long overdue. Ramón sought the Princess Alecia. There had been no sign of her or that rogue Vard Anton in eight months, despite the search parties, many of which had failed to return. In the early days, he had blamed Anton for the disappearance of the men, mainly mercenaries, who had been sent to find the princess, but then his own party had been attacked by elves and almost wiped out. Only he and Benae had survived that encounter.

Now there were rumors of attacks on outlying farmsteads. It didn't seem to be the work of the elves and mostly involved the death of livestock – chickens, sheep, goats, even the odd cow had been mauled or carried off. Some of the reports spoke of a fearsome creature, black and shaggy, part beast and part man, that raided their farms in the hours of darkness. There had even been word of the disappearance of a young woman from one of the remote holdings. Ramón didn't quite know what to make of it, but while he searched for Alecia, he'd keep his ears and eyes peeled for signs of the creature, and for the elves.

Alecia. He had once thought he loved her. He had been naive then, full of romantic notions about winning her hand in marriage. Foolish notions that Alecia had been right to reject. But he had grown into a man to be reckoned with in the eight months since her leaving. He had fallen in love, true love, with the woman Alecia always said would love him for himself: Benae, the mother of his unborn babe. The thought sent a shaft of unease into his heart. His baby but thought by the outside world to be that of the dead prince, Alecia's father. It was a necessary deception, but it galled Ramón that he couldn't shout the truth across the rooftops.

They *would* meet again; he knew it in his gut. He'd find Alecia and bring her back, but life would never be the same for the princess. Her father was dead and so was her betrothed. Benae, Alecia's stepmother, now held the power in Brightcastle. Yes, Alecia had a lot to grieve for and it was he, Ramón, who would have to break the ill tidings. But he would have none other take the duty.

Alecia would hardly recognize him when they met. No man in Brightcastle could now best him with the sword or the longbow. Practice at weapons had filled out his muscles, and now it was he the ladies watched, and he the young lads sought to emulate. He was now more than a match for Vard Anton.

Ramón couldn't believe he was finally on Alecia's trail after months of teeth-grinding frustration. The winter had kept him close to Brightcastle, and then when spring came Benae had been unwell, her pregnancy threatened. He resorted to advice from Hetty, and the witch had concocted a potion to stop Benae's body from flushing the child from her womb. He hadn't told Benae, just added a little of the mixture to her tea, night and morning. Benae would never have touched anything tainted by Hetty, blaming her as she did for Prince Zialni's demise. But finally, all was well and they looked forward to the birth in mid-autumn. There was plenty of time remaining for Ramón to find Alecia and return her to Brightcastle as the king had asked.

A farmstead appeared as they rounded a bend and Ramón reined in. Calling to his men to make a quick camp at the side of the road, he went on by himself and pulled up at the gate of the farmhouse. A woman in her later middle years swept the porch out the front, and a craggy-faced farmer stalked from the barn toward the woman. They stood, hands grasped together, and stared at him with suspicion.

Ramón climbed down from his horse and looped the reins over the gate post, adjusting his cloak and settling his sword more comfortably at his hip. His eyes sought the couple again, but they looked no more welcoming than before. Small wonder if they had been victims of raiders or dark elves. He gave his horse one last pat and pushed through the gate.

"Master, Mistress," he said, "I'm Ramón Zorba, the Guardian of Brightcastle. You may not be aware that the prince died back in winter and King Beniel has given stewardship of the principality to myself and the prince's widow."

Instead of smoothing his welcome, his words deepened the frowns of the couple before him.

"We have heard," the mistress said. "What do you want, Lord Zorba?"

Ramón couldn't help the rise of his eyebrows at the lack of respect. No introductions, no greeting, only suspicion. But at least they had heard of him.

"What I want is some respect from you. I've done you the courtesy of an introduction and I'd like to know to whom I speak." He was rather proud of the command of his words, but the farmer couple remained unmoved except for the mistress, who raised one eyebrow. The master looked as though he wished he had his axe to hand.

"You speak with Thom and Dana Andra," Mistress Andra said, "and I ask again the purpose of your visit."

Ramón sighed. It was against his nature to be abrupt, and it didn't seem to be working all that well with the Andras. "I know you've had difficult times here on the border and that breeds suspicion. Raiders and dark elves are no easy thing to overcome."

Master Andra scoffed. "You're not welcome here, Lord Zorba, but it's the fault of the late prince, not the times."

"You're Jorge Andra's parents?" Ramon had finally linked the couple with Jorge, the late squire of Brightcastle, who had returned to help his parents on their farm. He'd been killed when Prince Zialni ordered his mercenaries to collect more taxes from the farmers.

"That we are," the mistress said, "and we have no more sons to sacrifice to the kingdom." Mistress Andra broke in a sob and her husband pulled her face against his shoulder.

"I'm truly sorry for your loss," he said, looking into Thom Andra's eyes. What he saw tore at his soul, for exposed was the aching loss of an only son, a child made more precious by the extremes of life in this outpost. "You must realize that times have changed."

"We have no reason to trust you just because the prince and his lackey Finus are dead," Thom Andra said, rubbing a hand over his wife's shoulder. "Nothing will bring our son back."

Ramón bowed his head. Princess Alecia had avenged Jorge's death by killing at least three of the mercenaries involved, before being arrested and imprisoned. She had been disguised as a lad, and Ramón still couldn't quite believe Alecia had killed men in order to right the wrongs of her father. She had fled Brightcastle with the aid of Vard Anton and they had been on the run ever since.

"Nothing will bring Jorge back," said Ramón, "but I still need your help." Dana Andra gave a low snort, but Ramón pushed on regardless. "I've come to ask you some questions." He noted the heightened wariness on their faces. "Perhaps if we could go inside and have a pot of tea?"

"Any questions you have can be asked out here," Dana Andra said, her watery blue eyes snapping with anger.

Ramón quashed the irritation that bubbled up. "As you wish. I'm seeking the Princess Alecia. Do you know anything of her whereabouts?"

"No."

Alarm flared in the woman's eyes but was quickly suppressed, and Ramón wondered if he had imagined it.

"You've not seen or heard anything of her in the last eight months?"

They both shook their heads.

"We haven't seen her," Thom Andra said.

Ramón knew they were hiding something, but it would do no good to accuse them. "Well then, what of the tales of dark elves and this marauding creature?"

Thom Andra cleared his throat. "I myself have been accosted by the elves but it was back in the winter. Reminded me of the stories my grandfather used to tell. Do you think they're planning an invasion?"

"I fear that could be so," Ramón said, not wanting to get distracted by talk of the elves. "We've had trouble in the east last spring, but the elves were driven back into the north. We'll deal with them if they come again. They have ever been disorganized rabble and should pose no great threat."

Thom Andra laughed. "You've heard different to me then, young lord."

"Regardless," Ramón said, gritting his teeth, "do you have any information on this creature that's attacking outlying farms? It's said to be large and wolf-like and has been responsible for stock losses. There is also a young woman missing."

"Nothing like that has troubled us," Thom Andra said. "Now if you'd allow, we need to return to our chores."

Without further words of farewell, the couple departed, leaving Ramón staring at their retreating backs.

"Yes, of course," he said, though they hadn't waited for his agreement. They were hiding something, but what? Knowledge of Princess Alecia? That had to be it, for nothing else explained their behavior. His pulse quickened. This was the closest he'd come to gaining any information on her disappearance. Brightcastle had been bled dry of mercenaries in the hunt for the princess, but now he, Ramón, would return her to her rightful place. He could see the crowds now as they rode into Brightcastle, but better than acclamation would be the undying gratitude of the king.

Ramón turned and strode to his horse, mounted and rode back to his soldiers. He joined them in an early luncheon after which they continued up the road past the farmhouse. He felt the suspicious eyes of the Andras as he led his men into the forest. Out of sight of the farm, Ramón drew rein.

"Stay here," he said, dismounting. "I'm going to circle back and take a closer look at the property."

He tossed his reins to his second-in-command and entered the forest that lay between them and the Andra farm. Soon the smoke from the farmhouse could be seen through the trees and he slowed, making his way cautiously to the rear of the property. He snagged his cloak on a bush as he crept through the sparse undergrowth and cursed.

The farmhouse came into view and he spied a neat vegetable garden laid out behind. Rows of plants waved in the slight breeze and ears of corn appeared almost ready to harvest. As he stared at the peaceful scene, he saw a woman amidst the plants, her head bent at some task. Who was she? The Andras had not mentioned anyone else living at the farm, though he hadn't asked.

There was something familiar about her, something in the tilt of her head and the angle of her shoulders that nagged at him. She wore a red dress patterned with small white flowers, and an old straw bonnet protected her face from the sun, and from his questing gaze. A thick blonde plait poked from under the back of the bonnet and was tied with a lilac ribbon. He crept closer, determined to speak to the woman and ask if she knew anything about Princess Alecia.

He had approached to within ten paces of the garden fence when the woman stood up and he observed she was heavily pregnant. She arched her back, massaging the muscles there, and then bringing her hands across her belly to rub its swollen mass. Ramón was no judge of these things, but she seemed very close to her full term. She looked down at her stomach and appeared to speak to it. He felt shame intruding on such a private moment between the woman and her unborn child, but he couldn't take his eyes from the picture she made.

The woman chose that moment to lift her head and stare northward and he gasped, staggering back several steps. His heart raced away; palms immediately slick as he stared at the face of Alecia Zialni.

Her eyes widened as she discovered herself under scrutiny. There was a nerve-wrenching moment as both stared, Ramón's eyes trapped by the startled lilac gaze of the woman he had loved and lost to Vard Anton.

"Ramón!" she said, her throat working as though she swallowed hard. "What are you doing here?"

"What am *I* doing here?" he said. "What are you doing here, and in *that* condition?" He couldn't help the surge of fury that coursed through his gut. How often had he dreamed of this moment over the last eight months? Dreamed of the moment when he would rescue the princess from the clutches of the outlaw Anton? Alecia had never looked like this in his dream: her stomach swollen with child, hands grubby from labor in the earth, clothes unlike any she had ever worn. "Who has done this to you, or do I even have to ask?"

Her chin came up in the familiar pose of anger. "It's none of your concern."

He couldn't bear the frostiness in her voice. "I've come to take you home."

She laughed, without mirth. "I'm not going anywhere like this," she said. "I wouldn't risk the babe, and I can't return to my father when he has treated me with such disregard."

"Princess," he said, stepping closer, "your father is dead. He passed away suddenly last winter."

Alecia stared at him and then seemed to sway. Ramon reached for her and pulled her against him. Her belly brushed his arm. She pushed away from him, rather harder than expected, and he nearly fell on his backside. Her lilac gaze accused him.

"There must be some misunderstanding," she said, in the haughty tone he well remembered. "My father can't be dead."

Ramón paused, searching for words, but there were none that could make this easier. "I'm sorry, Princess, but the prince *is* dead and his wife, Princess Benae, is in charge of Brightcastle. The king has granted me the task of aiding the princess, as she is also with child."

"He isn't dead. I would have known," she snapped, her hands clasped over her abdomen. "And as for this Princess Benae, I'll *never* accept her. I see by your attitude she has you in her thrall."

"These words don't become you," he said, feeling his face flush. Damn but she could still make him feel like a clumsy squire!

"Show me his body and I will believe!"

"Princess, please!" Ramón said. "You know I have your best interests at heart. I've cared for Brightcastle and its people in your absence and since we lost His Highness. You know how highly I held your father. I would've done anything to be able to return you to him. He died in his bed, suddenly, and the physician declared natural causes. His body lies at Wildecoast in the family crypt."

Alecia covered her face with her hands, shoulders slumped, and Ramón approached once again. He placed a hand on her shoulder and offered her a handkerchief, which she pressed to her eyes.

"I'm sorry, Princess, this can't be easy to hear," he said, shifting his hand to her back and rubbing in circles, just as Benae liked when she was upset.

Alecia stepped away from him, blew her nose, and then fixed her hard lilac gaze on him. "I know you wouldn't lie to me, Ramón, and so I must believe your words, even though they break my heart." Her voice broke. "I loved him."

She buried her face in the handkerchief once more and her shoulders shook. She was a picture of vulnerability. His heart ached that he had been the one to devastate her with news of her loss.

"Your father loved you and he wanted you back. I promised myself I'd make his wish come true and here I am."

"He wanted me back so I could produce an heir for the kingdom. Well, Ramón," she said, running her hands over her abdomen. "What do you think he'd say to *this* heir?"

"Don't be ridiculous," he said, grasping Alecia's hands in his. "*That* child cannot be heir."

She had spoilt everything with her vendetta. Why did she have to take it upon herself to avenge the death of the Andra's son? Why did she have to flee with Anton instead of allowing him to help her out of her troubles? Her stomach brushed his knuckles and disgust swamped him. He dropped her hands and ran his fingers through his hair. "Why have you done this? I'll kill Anton. I'll find him and kill him. Where is he?"

She sighed, her arms wrapped protectively about her belly. "I don't know where he is. I've not seen him since the winter. He doesn't know about the child."

"Then it *is* his?"

"Of course it is. Do you think so little of me that you imagine I would lie with any man?"

Ramón shook his head. "I no longer know what to think. You've done a magnificent job of ruining your life."

"I was left with few choices. What would you have done?"

"It doesn't have to be that way anymore. Finus is dead."

Her chin came up. "So it's true? Finus died of his wounds?"

"He died a month after the wounds inflicted the night you fled with Anton. His death was slow and at the end, he asked for your forgiveness."

Alecia snorted. "I'll *never* forgive him. I'm glad he's dead. He was at the root of all that was evil in Brightcastle."

She had changed in more ways than just her pregnancy. How had his Alecia grown into this hard woman who no longer trusted? Ramón almost gasped out loud as he realized what he had thought. *His Alecia.* She wasn't his, not anymore. He had thought those feelings long dead but the woman before him still had a hold over his heart, despite the fact he had a wife waiting for him.

"Princess, all that's left to restore Brightcastle is your return. Much has changed and the kingdom needs you." He studied the effect his words had on her, a mixture of hope and despair. "Please come home."

"Curious that you would wish me back when you have such a cozy arrangement with Princess Benae," Alecia said. "Or did I misinterpret your feelings for her?"

His face heated for the second time. "You didn't misinterpret. Benae is the woman you always said I'd find."

Her eyes narrowed as if she was only just seeing Ramón. "You've changed," she said, walking around him and stopping to peer up into his eyes. "Your shoulders have broadened, and your eyes are no longer… innocent. You move with assurance and grace and… danger. I'm glad you're happy, but your position as lover to the princess will make it hard for our friendship. I'll never accept her."

"I'm her husband and joint steward of Brightcastle, appointed by the king himself, and you *will* accept Benae. You have no choice."

"We shall see."

"Come back with me, Princess. We'll enter Brightcastle under cover of darkness and hide you away until the babe is born. One of the maids can raise it and you'll be free to be the princess once again." He took her hands in his, willing her to see sense.

"You talk of my child as if I can just cast him off," she said, dragging her hands free. "Part of me is in this child. Why would I want to disown him, no matter how I feel about his father?"

"Did he rape you?"

"Ramón!" Her face colored and her eyes dropped from his.

"Tell me what happened, Alecia. Did he hurt you?"

She turned toward the farmhouse. "This is none of your business."

"I *will* kill him. I'll track him down and kill him, I vow."

Alecia kept walking toward the house, and he followed. She spun to face him. "Leave now. I'll send word when I'm ready to return, but I'll never pretend this child isn't mine."

Her words stung him and yet again he realized Alecia had integrity he could never claim. *She* would never disown her child, no matter what the populace thought of her.

"You think I can leave now, knowing where you are?"

"I'm not returning with you."

"Then I'll bring the king here and he'll convince you."

"You'll do no such thing!" she said, lilac eyes full of determination. "I'll deliver my babe, and, after a suitable recovery, we'll return to Brightcastle. And we shall see who is mistress thereafter."

The door swung open and Mistress Andra stood with her arms crossed. "What's the meaning of all this yelling? Alecia, you should know better than to get yourself worked up like this. It's not good for the babe."

Ramón frowned and chewed his lip, but Alecia blushed deeply. "I'm sorry, Dana." She turned to Ramón. "This is Lord Ramón of Brightcastle."

"We've met, and the last time we talked, Lord Zorba was headed north." She turned her eyes to Ramón. "You're now trespassing, Sir."

"Never mind," Alecia said. "He was just leaving."

"Oh no I'm not, Princess. I meant what I said."

Alecia looked at him with exasperation, but Mistress Andra frowned and stepped backward across the threshold. "You'd better come inside."

CHAPTER 17

ALECIA'S belly went rock hard as she waddled over to take a seat at the kitchen table. She breathed deeply, trying to disguise her discomfort, but Dana wasn't fooled. She laid her palm on Alecia's abdomen, feeling for the contractions.

"All will be well," she said. "Your body prepares for the birth."

"I wish to take her back to Brightcastle," Ramón said. "The midwife there can manage her."

Alecia frowned at his tentative smile. He didn't care for the babe, only to get her back within his world. She studied her old friend, noticing the subtle difference life had wrought over the past seasons. He had grown in stature and confidence, and the quiet light of assurance glowed in his gaze. He believed in himself now, and Alecia knew he would be difficult to refuse.

Dana said. "The trip could kill her or the babe or both. It can't be risked."

Again, there was a tension around Dana's eyes that spoke to Alecia of some worry she held. Pain stabbed through her lower abdomen and she gasped and clutched her stomach. Was the babe coming now? She cried out as another spasm, worse than the first, hit her.

She felt herself lifted and carried into her bedroom, laid gently on the bed. Dana's hands ran over her stomach, pressing hard against the child. Alecia groaned. "Make the pain go away."

Dana left and Ramón's fingers clutched at hers, squeezing tight, his warmth comforting. "I won't leave you, Alecia. I was mad to agree last time."

She shook her head, but another pain hit and by the time it passed, Dana was back with her potion. She drank, propped against the pillows with Dana's arm around her shoulders. A warm wave of lethargy seeped over her making her blessedly sleepy. The last thing she remembered was Dana slipping her arm free and the covers being drawn up to her chin.

* * *

Ramón closed the door of the bedroom quietly and watched Dana Andra as she paced across the living room, a frown on her brow.

"What's wrong?"

"Perhaps nothing," Dana answered, still pacing.

He stepped before her. "Tell me."

She looked up at him. "You truly care for the princess?"

"I'd do anything for her."

"I've birthed dozens of babes and I believe this child lies bottom down. He can't be born that way and his position causes the pain the princess suffers."

Ramón frowned, a tendril of fear curling around his gut. He couldn't lose Alecia now he had found her! "I'll take her to Brightcastle. There'll be someone who can help her.

"She can't be moved." Dana wrung her hands. "You saw her. It would be agony."

"Dosed up with your potion I could get her there."

"No." Dana's voice was flat, uncompromising.

He drew himself up. No mere farmwife was going to stand in his way. "You have no say in the matter, Mistress. If you don't feel competent to deliver this child and save Alecia, I must find someone who can."

"Then find someone, but she stays here."

Master Andra appeared in the doorway with his short bow, an arrow trained at Ramón's chest. "I don't want to shoot you, boy, but use that tone with my wife again and I will. The princess goes nowhere."

He stared into the farmer's eyes, seeing the steely determination that allowed him to survive in this hostile land. Perhaps they were right. It might kill Alecia to move her now. Another solution must be found. He slapped his palm against the wall in frustration.

"Where can I go for help?"

At that moment Alecia screamed and they all turned toward the bedroom. Dana stopped Ramón when he would have entered. "Let me talk to her," she said. "It's time I spoke the truth."

* * *

Fear took Alecia's breath. What Dana said couldn't be true. But the pain! She'd die if she had to face much more of this. "Are you certain these aren't birth pains? Perhaps there's nothing wrong."

Dana smiled and Alecia hated the sympathy in the woman's gaze. She felt tears smart her own eyes.

"It's not your time yet, Alecia. Your pains are a sign the babe isn't resting as he should be. You're in your last month and he should be ready for birth. Instead he sits head upright. I can't bring him into the world as he is."

"Might he not turn of his own accord?"

"He might."

"But you don't think he will."

"I pray to the Goddess every night that all will be well and that I'll deliver you a healthy baby."

Alecia swallowed, her throat thick with fear. "I'm not ready for death yet, Dana." She thought of Vard never knowing his child, not even knowing he had a child and realized that her babe's life was more important than her own. An idea grew in her mind, one that would ensure the survival of her child and provide protection for him. She fixed her gaze upon Dana and took a deep breath.

"When the babe comes, if he's still breech and cannot be born, you must cut him from my body."

Dana gasped and clutched her hands. "No, Princess. I won't do it. Don't ask it of me."

Ramón pushed into the room, his face incredulous. "How can you say such a thing to Mistress Andra?" His blue gaze accused her and anger stood in every line of his body. "You won't throw your life away."

She struggled to sit up in the bed and pulled the covers over her naked belly. Ramón had hate in his eyes and it seemed directed at her child, at her gravid stomach. "If it appears the situation is hopeless then Dana must do as I say. At least the child will survive, and even I may have a chance."

"No," he said, the sound like the single drum stroke after a death. "You'll have no chance. You'll die, and I won't allow it."

"Better that than lose us both."

"No!" Ramón advanced on the bed, rage contorting his features. "My sister was in just exactly this position when she labored with my nephew. The surgeon thought he could cut the babe from her womb. The child was already dead and I watched my sister die from blood loss. Do you know how that feels?"

Alecia felt an answering grief within her. "Yes, I know how it feels to watch a loved one die," she said quietly, suddenly calm and sure of her decision. "If I am to die, I still want my child to know life." She stared up at Ramón. "And to know his father."

"No!" he said. "That bastard has done enough. He has no place in your life."

She reached for his hand. "I need him, Ramón."

"No."

"I need him, and so does this child. Please, I need to see him one more time. Think of it as a last request."

Ramón covered his face in his hands, his shoulders trembling. Alecia felt miserable at having to use him like this, but realization of her mortality crystallized her focus. Vard was out there somewhere and this child needed him. *She* needed him even if it was merely to hold her hand as she died. "Find him for me, Ramón, and bring him here."

His head snapped up; eyes wide. "If I find him, I'll kill him," he ground out.

"No, you won't," she said, gently. "I know you'd do anything for me. I believe in our friendship. Remember that when you find Vard and do as I ask." She knew he couldn't resist her request.

"I'll find him if I can."

She drew him closer. "I know you'll succeed. He told me he was heading east but I don't know if he did. I have dark dreams and I think Vard… I think he may be changed." She couldn't reveal Vard's secret, but neither could she send Ramón out there unprepared.

"You think he's insane?"

"Just be careful. I see you are changed as well, and I think you're the man for the task."

He raised his head, eyes full of pride. Alecia wished she deserved the smile that lit his blue eyes. She could only hope he'd find Vard, that he was equal to the task of finding the only man she had ever loved. Ramón and Vard would ensure her child lived, and one day someone would tell him of her gift of life. She smiled up at him. He kissed her forehead with a gentle brush of his lips and left the room.

Chapter 18

RAMÓN sat by his fire, the morning cold for the summer season, sipping the last of his breakfast tea and mulling over the previous two weeks. The flames entranced him, for he hoped to see in their dancing brightness a vision that would tell him where his search lay. Time was running out, but he felt closer to his quarry by the day. Searching for the father of Alecia's babe had truly been like trying to find a speck of gold in all the sand of Wildecoast, but as he talked to farmers and loggers and read the signs of the forest, he had started to piece together a picture. He didn't like it.

Alecia's parting words echoed in his mind – *he may be changed.* Ramón thought he knew what the princess had hinted at, though he didn't want to believe it. Over the last two weeks he had ranged far and wide, sending his men across the area to gather information on the movements of strangers, dark elves and bandits. What he heard concerned him and would upset the king. There was certainly activity by the dark elves when it was thought they had retreated far to the north.

Bandits were no more an issue than they had always been, but a dark creature of some type, or maybe more than one, plagued the countryside over a wide area. Descriptions varied, but always the howling was mentioned. Man, monster or wolf, a creature stalked the people of these outlying farms and homesteads. There had been livestock taken, and Ramón now camped in an area where an attack had occurred the night before last. All reports said the livestock they found were mutilated, the flesh torn by giant teeth. In the last attack a huge black wolf had knocked a farmer down as he beat his son for disobedience. The man was shaken but uninjured. Ramón was secretly glad he had been so punished for the treatment of his son.

No matter the information he had gathered, Ramón knew he would have to head back to the Andras soon and didn't want to go empty-handed. Alecia's time was running out, and if this pregnancy must result in her death, he wished to see her one last time.

The hairs on the back of his neck stirred and he looked around the tiny clearing, trying to discover the cause of his unease.

Movement stirred at the edge of his vision. He turned as a man in ragged clothes hurtled into him and knocked him flat, before spinning to face him from mere paces away. Ramón sprang to his feet and drew his sword, waving it at the interloper. His attacker was tall with black hair that hung in dirty locks halfway down his chest. A thick beard covered his face and his eyes were feral… and familiar! Gold-flecked green eyes glared at Ramón out of that hairy face, eyes he hadn't seen in more than eight months.

Excitement coursed through his veins, the beating of his heart loud in his ears. Anton snarled as if he were about to leap upon him again. "Captain Anton, it's Ramón Zorba," he said, tensed for Anton's attack. "I must take you to the princess."

The captain cocked his head to the side as if hearing something familiar, at least Ramón hoped that was the case. Perhaps if he kept talking?

"The princess is in trouble and wants to see you, nay, must see you. She's dying." Saying the words made Alecia's situation all the more real. Ramón had not admitted his fear, even to himself. He was a coward, and her courage and sacrifice shamed him.

But now wasn't the time for recriminations. He raised his voice, a surge of anger at the unfairness of life striking him. "I said, she is dying."

Anton snarled at the words and launched himself at Ramón, his human teeth bared and the nails on his fingertips poised to rake his skin. Ramón pulled out of a sword stroke that would've killed his attacker and instead hit him in the side of the head with the flat of the blade. Anton was deflected sideways by the blow and fell to the earth on the other side of the fire pit, shaking his head, eyes unfocused.

"Come, man," Ramón said. "Will that be enough to knock some sense into you? I haven't the time to waste fighting." It surprised him he truly felt little fear, a far cry from the man who lost Alecia to Vard in the first place.

Anton snarled and leapt for him again and this time Ramón wasn't quick enough to block the charge. He was knocked to the ground, his opponent's fingers closing around his neck. He promptly returned the favor, squeezing the hard muscles of Vard's throat with his own hands. This close, he could see the man was insane, the feral gleam of his golden irises convincing Ramón he was fighting for his life. He wouldn't let this beast win! He had to return to Alecia, with or without Vard Anton. Desperation gave him strength, and he brought his knee up hard between Anton's legs to crush his manhood. Hot breath whooshed from his mouth and his eyes rolled up in his head before he rolled off Ramón, hands grasping his genitals. Ramón wasted no time, reaching for his sword and smashing it down upon Anton's temple. He slumped, his face gone slack and blood rushing from a wound near his left ear.

Ramón stood over him, shoulders heaving. Had he inflicted a mortal wound? He thought back to the night in the garden when his hired assassin had shot Anton twice with a crossbow. He had survived that, so a bump to the head should be nothing. The temptation to finish the task swept over him and he raised his sword, imagining Anton's head sliced clean from his shoulders. But the memory of Alecia's shining face, full of trust, filled his mind and he lowered the blade. Vard Anton might not survive the journey back, but at least Alecia could see him one last time. Ramón bound his hands and feet and slung him over his horse.

By the time Ramón stopped for the midday meal, his captive was awake and snarling fit to burst. Raven snorted and pranced with every sound Anton made, and finally Ramón was forced to pull him from his mount to avoid an accident. He would have laughed if it were not so tragic.

The brave and handsome Captain Vard Anton had been reduced to a savage animal, clad in rags, bound hand and foot because he couldn't be trusted to act like a civilized human being. It was not only tragic but concerning. Ramón couldn't bring him before Alecia like this. She would simply not cope while in such a terrible state herself.

He grabbed another rope and tied Anton to a tree. His eyes were glazed and unfocused but at least he had survived his capture, which was more than he deserved, in Ramón's opinion. But how was he to prepare the man for presentation to the princess? It was a hopeless cause, far better to knock him on the head and present the body. But would Alecia accept his death wasn't Ramón's fault? She was stubborn and in love with this animal, and on top of that she was hardly likely to be rational when in such pain. That was if she still lived. Anything could have occurred in the weeks he'd been gone.

He shook his head as he stared down at his captive. What manner of creature was this before him? What had befallen him that he had sunk this low? The feral eyes with their golden specks glinted at him, nothing but malice in their depths.

"You've lost everything you ever had, Anton," he said, squatting just out of reach, his sword across his legs. "And because of your actions, Alecia might very well lose her life. The Princess Alecia. Does that mean anything to you?"

He paused to judge the effect of his words, but aside from a narrowing of eyes, there was no change to the snarling expression. "Princess Alecia could be dying," he shouted. "I'm taking you to her, but she can't see you in this condition."

Despair swept like a cold wind through his heart and he shuddered. He didn't want to be in this position, dealing with a madman, Alecia's life hanging in the balance. He wanted to be by her side, to bring her babe into the world, and to hold its mother's hand perhaps for the last time in life. What good could this animal possibly be in that situation? Even more, he wished to be back with Benae, to know she was safe and that their child was too.

He turned away in disgust and dug a small fire pit. Once a pot of water was heating over the flames, he dug dried beef and a hard knob of cheese from his pack and offered them one at a time to Anton on a stick. He took them in his teeth and ate them, a frown creasing his brow. Ramón didn't understand. Anton's mind had snapped under the Goddess only knew what forces, and Ramón was not equal to the task of healing the shreds of Anton's sanity. He didn't even *want* to heal the man.

The pot boiled and Ramón made tea. The aromatic liquid lent its scent to the pines of the clearing and Anton's nose twitched. Perhaps the more familiar sights, sounds and aromas of human habitation could bring him back from wherever it was he dwelt. Ramón sat across the fire from Anton and sang the lullaby that most kingdom babes had crooned to them in the cradle. It wasn't a tuneful rendition, but Anton relaxed a little. The song finished and the men sat staring at each other, Ramón at a loss as to what to do now.

Perhaps conversation could help. "I've been sent by Princess Alecia to bring you back to her, Anton." The eyes narrowed again. "She loves you; the Goddess knows why. But I'll not be able to bring you before her like this. Do you remember Alecia?"

The muscles of Anton's throat moved convulsively. "Alecia?" he croaked, more of a growl than words, but Ramón understood. Perhaps a spark of humanity remained. His stomach clenched at the thought of this *dog* beside Alecia's bed.

"Yes, Alecia. She loves you and needs you back."

He stood to emphasize his point and Anton lurched backward snarling. Ramón instantly went still, hands outstretched, eyes lowered. "I won't hurt you unless I have to." Was that true? "But I can't let her see you like this. You must remember Alecia."

He seated himself slowly, eyes still lowered, and began crooning the lullaby once more, the nursery song foreign in the wilderness. When he dared look up again, he found Anton observing him with eyes that seemed a little more human than they had moments before.

Ramón stood and readied for departure. He untied Anton from the tree and tethered the rope to his black mare. He mounted and moved out of the clearing, Anton following, his posture crouched over his hands. It was all Ramón could do to control his horse. Raven snorted and fussed, starting forward, only to pull up and then start forward again. He couldn't understand it, but then observed the horse's reaction when Vard happened to touch its tail. Raven trembled so much Ramón was sure she'd collapse.

He halted. Clearly, Raven perceived Vard Anton to be a threat. He unsettled the horse worse than anything Ramón had yet encountered. Raven was accustomed to boar and lion hunts and was even battle trained. Ramón shook his head, wondering at the true state of his prisoner. Was this just insanity, or something else entirely? He looked at Vard Anton who straightened his posture, meeting his open stare with challenge in his gaze.

"Come, we must continue." Ramón turned forward. "I'll talk as we ride."

They journeyed thus for the remainder of the day, Ramón talking and singing soldiering songs of battle and swordfights and glory, Vard seeming to grow more human and less animal as the afternoon wore on. But at last the day took its toll and he could go no further. He slumped behind Raven, and the mare snorted and reared, causing Ramón to nearly lose his seat.

"May as well stop here," he said, dismounting and tying Anton's rope to the nearest tree. Anton groaned and rolled closer to the tree to take the pressure off his wrists. "Are you well, man?" Ramón asked.

Anton looked at him. "My head aches." His voice was still croaky, but he made more sense than he had in a while.

Ramón found a shred of pity within him. He had hit his head exceedingly hard and then forced the man to trek all day. Small wonder he was in poor condition. "I'll prepare some food and you'll feel better. Here," he handed him a cup of water, "this will help."

Anton downed the water as if it were his last drink and closed his eyes. Ramón watched, wondering if he had pushed him too hard. What if he came this far only to lose his prisoner? He shook his head at his folly and prepared the cold meal.

***

Vard's head pounded as they sat gnawing at the dried beef and hard cheese. This man had caused the injury to his head. He thought fleetingly that it would be pleasing to have the soft flesh of that tanned throat between his jaws. He shook the thought away and was rewarded with a crushing ache in his skull. The numbing fog that had encased his thoughts over the past weeks had lifted somewhat but he couldn't remember what had brought him to this place, this situation. The blond man before him looked familiar, but Vard couldn't place him either.

The man who called himself Ramón cleared his throat. "I'm taking you to see Alecia. She carries your child and is due any day. You do remember the princess, don't you?"

A small frown creased Vard's brow. The name of the woman caused a sharp pang of sorrow within him. He didn't know if he wished to remember. "Describe her to me." His voice was still gravelly after the long weeks of misuse, his throat sore.

"She's beautiful, tall, with long blonde hair. A buxom lass with a smile that lights her face. I can't believe you could have forgotten her. Here, I have her likeness painted on the cover of my flint box."

Ramón pulled a small metal box from his vest. A girl with long fair hair and lilac eyes smiled at Vard from the lid. Ramón was right, her smile did light her face and her eyes. . . He had known eyes like that but it felt like another life away. He stared at the picture until Ramón put the box back in his pocket.

What had he said? She was with child? His child? He stared at his captor and watched him tense, his right hand reaching for his sword. Vard tried not to glare so hard. "You said she was with child?"

"Don't you remember anything? This is important, man!"

"Answer my question."

"Yes, I said she was with child and it's yours. She may be dying as we speak. The babe is breech and the midwife has said she can't deliver it. Alecia has decreed that it must be cut from her, and if that happens, she'll die."

"You sound very sure."

"I know she can't survive a knife in the belly. She'll lose too much blood. I saw it happen to my own sister."

Vard thought of those lilac eyes and suddenly the memory of a girl in a cream gown at a ball came to him.

"You remember something." Ramón leaned forward, the light of triumph in his gaze.

"Yes, a ball and… Alecia… in a cream gown."

"That was the night of her betrothal." A shadow crossed his face as though the recollection was unpleasant. "I've never seen her more beautiful, but it was the beginning of all this in a way."

Vard closed his eyes against the confusing words. All he wanted was to be left alone with his pain, not to be dragged across the countryside to see some girl who declared he was her babe's father. But there was that tantalizing glimpse of a beautiful woman and then… Fear? Fear in those lilac eyes, in a garden at night. Fear that he would attack her. It was a different memory, more distant, and seen through a mist.

Something clicked in his skull and he stepped closer to the events of the past, a pace closer to a life he didn't think he wanted to reclaim. There was pain there, the pain of loss, of death, of betrayal, and the certainty his life would mean another's death, over and again. He shook his head and rolled his back to Ramón. "I'll sleep now."

The morning brought a cool wind and rain that swept at Vard from dark clouds. His sleep had been restless, full of accusing violet eyes, the face of a dark sorcerer, the fear of death, and worse. His shoulder and side ached upon waking, and when he pulled his tunic up a healed wound throbbed at his waist. Vard found he could finally remember the event that had caused his injuries.

He heard a sudden intake of breath and looked across the campfire to find Ramón staring at his scar. "What the devil?"

Vard pulled his tunic down over the wound. Why did it still ache? "A fight some time back. I sought help from a sorcerer who then betrayed me. He's now dead."

"You can remember?"

"Some."

"You remember Alecia?"

"Some, enough to know she won't want to see me." His voice was smoother today but his mood was still rough, still full of the discomfort of not knowing his place.

"You are the father of her child."

Ramón's low words, delivered with quiet intensity, assailed him, made him feel he had been dropped from a height and landed on his head. "I don't know the truth anymore."

"You're saying you don't believe her?"

Ramón was too indignant. Did he love the princess? Vard seemed to remember a younger man with stars in his eyes. Could the princess have put them there?

"Goddess!" Ramón said, leaping to his feet as if he'd defend Alecia's honor on the spot. "She wouldn't lie about such a thing."

"She would if she didn't know she was lying, if she didn't know she had been with another man. That sorcerer implied intimate knowledge of the princess. Perhaps the babe is his?"

"No." Ramón shook his head, the thick blond locks sweeping across his eyes.

Vard almost smiled. This man was far more deserving of Alecia's regard than he was, and yet she had clearly seen him as a friend, not a lover. A sharp picture of Ramón trying to force himself on Alecia in the garden the night of her betrothal came to Vard and he hesitated. The jumbled images in his mind didn't make sense. His head ached, and all he wished for was a soft bed and to be left alone. "I can't deal with this now."

"That is not an option. Another day and we'll reach the farm where the princess now resides. You must prepare to meet her and to accept what you see. Tell me how you'll do this."

"How can I do that when I don't know myself, literally. I can see you love the princess. Why would you bring me to her to complicate matters?"

"I once loved her, but I've made a life of my own with a wonderful woman. Now all I feel for her is loyalty and friendship, just as she always wanted. She charged me with bringing you to her because she knows she may die, and she wishes to see you; for you to know your child. I know she loves you. Did you *ever* love her?"

"My memory is still hazy, jumbled. The strongest feeling is guilt. I've done something to her which I don't believe she can forgive, but I can't remember what. I think I must have loved her once but perhaps it doesn't matter now. Perhaps she would be better off without me?"

Ramón stared. "I won't argue against that, but Alecia wants to see you and I can't ignore her request. I can't understand why she loves you, but she does."

Vard laid his head against the tree behind him and closed his eyes. "Leave me here and return to her. She'll be happier in every way without me."

Ramón shook his head, but his expression showed torment. "There's nothing I'd like better, but I gave my solemn promise I'd find you and bring you to her."

"You can't be blamed if I won't return."

"Don't tempt me!"

Word by word, Vard's memory was returning, and he could clearly measure Ramón's growth over the past months. The naïve young man had become a formidable adversary, and his loyalty to the princess was unwavering. But could he leave his love to the protection of this man?

Shock robbed him of breath. *His love! Love...* The word resonated deep within. In a rush, all his memories flooded back, along with the feelings, good and bad.

Alecia was indeed his love, and more precious to him than his own life. It was why he had left her, so she could be safe - from him.

But he had to see her one last time. To hold her in his arms and tell her he loved her. From what Ramón said, it could be the last time she'd hear that in this life. Goddess! She might already be dead.

Vard met Ramón's gaze, not flinching from the angry light that blazed there. "I remember all that has passed between Alecia and myself. She is precious to me beyond all imagining."

Ramón snorted. "That's why you abandoned her, leaving her to bear her child alone?"

"I didn't know about the child! How could I?"

"What do you intend now? Are you man enough to face her? Knowing you brought about her ruin?"

Vard allowed the words to make their full mark, to score the wounds so clearly intended. He deserved no less after his behavior. "I'll return with you and speak to Alecia. I owe her that."

"You owe her that and more than you can *ever* repay." Ramón's anger accused him, made him ashamed. The squire that Vard had so easily dismissed had proved to be more of a man than he ever could. He'd have been a worthy husband for Alecia.

He faced Ramón squarely, so he'd know he could trust the words he needed to say. "Can you take care of her, Ramón?"

"What do you think I'm trying to do?"

"No. I mean, pick up where I left off. Save her. Take care of the child. All the things I won't be able to do."

Ramón shook his head. "I'd gladly do so but you're not making sense. You said you'd return."

Vard nodded. "Yes, and I will, but I can't stay. I'd put them at risk. They'll need a good man to care for them."

Ramón flinched as if the words hurt him. "A good man, you say."

"Yes, that's you. I see that now."

"No. If Alecia were to know everything about me, she'd hate me."

Vard shook his head. "We're not speaking of your sins but mine."

Ramón looked at him and Vard saw fear. "Have you ever ordered a man assassinated?"

"No, but I've killed several."

"I have paid with my own money to have a man killed," Ramón said, his eyes downcast. He looked back at Vard. "You. I ordered that assassin in the garden that night."

Vard pulled the memory from the depths of the fog that had enveloped his brain over the past weeks. "So that was your doing. Why?" He couldn't be angry with Ramón, not after all that had passed.

"Jealousy. I knew Alecia had feelings for you that she didn't have for me. I thought perhaps with you out of the way she'd transfer that regard to me. If she discovers what I've done, she'll hate me."

"What you did was stupid in the extreme. Do you know how close she came to dying that night?"

"I know she could have easily been killed by those darts," Ramón said. "Perhaps one day I'll be able to reveal my part in that night, but not now. She'd never understand."

"I'm content to leave it thus as long as you can promise to care for her when I'm gone."

"If she survives the birth, I'll care for both and see the princess happily married. You need have no fear for her."

Vard smiled through his pain, knowing Alecia might have the chance for happiness with another man. It wouldn't be with him, but she had never had the chance of happiness with him. He reached out and shook Ramón's hand, approving of the strength and certainty he felt in the other's grip.

CHAPTER 19

A LECIA screamed the sound of a wild animal in torment. The stabbing pain in her abdomen faded slowly to a dull ache and she rested her head back on the pillow, looking across at Dana. She looked almost as exhausted as Alecia felt, and worry enhanced the fine lines beside her eyes. She sat in a chair beside the bed and a large knife lay on the bedside table. Dana's eyes kept returning to the knife, and each time they did she trembled.

Sometime within the last sixteen hours of labor, Alecia had released her fear of death. It would be an escape from the pain she felt with each contraction. The babe should have been born long ago, and Dana had declared his life at risk if he wasn't born soon.

She had indeed been right about his position. Only his little bottom showed in her birth canal, and Dana had applied all her skill to try to push him away so she could seize his feet. But her efforts had been in vain. Alecia's body persisted in trying to force the babe from her womb even though it was an impossible feat. Soon they would have no choice but to cut it from her belly.

It might already be too late.

Where was Vard? She must see him before she died. She must tell him of the child and extract from him a promise to look after it. Now it was too late. He'd never arrive before her life blood drained away. Already Dana rose to insert the knife into the fire.

Fear returned to Alecia, stabbing through her heart and into her abdomen to join the agony already there. "I'm not ready, Dana," she said. "Hold my hand."

She turned, stark pity and fear in her gaze. "I wish there was more I could do, Alecia, but the time we had is spent, and now action must be taken or both of you will die."

She reached out and took Alecia's hand in hers. Alecia could feel the rough calluses from long days of work on the farm.

"I'll be quick," Dana said. "Perhaps heating the knife will stop some of the blood loss. I'll call Thom. He can hold the babe while I sew."

"Give the babe to me, Dana. I must hold him once before I die."

Dana stared at her as though she couldn't believe what she heard, what she must do. She nodded. "I'll give him to you if you're conscious, but Thom must be ready."

Alecia shook her head. Surely it wouldn't be that quick? She wouldn't die as soon as her womb was opened. She'd have hours to hold her young one before her last breath. She agreed anyway.

"After the next contraction, I'll perform the cut. You'll soon hold your babe. I'll fetch Thom."

Dana was back in moments, her frightened husband at her heels, looking like he'd rather be anywhere but here.

"Give her your knife, Thom. She can bite down on the handle now, and later when I cut."

Her husband handed his knife to Alecia reluctantly, his eyes wide.

"Grasp her shoulders when the contraction passes and hold her still."

The contraction hit and Alecia bit down on the wood, her scream gurgling past the handle, saliva dripping down her chin. She didn't want to die, wasn't ready after all to give her life for her child. Who could be ready for a thing like that? She had much life to live. She would not be a corpse, cold in the grave, her life cut short and a child left to wonder what could have been. *Vard where are you? Ramón why did you let me down?* Pain tore at her abdomen and she felt the dark edge of oblivion calling. She could fight no more. Terror that they might have left the cut too late swept over her and her gaze sought Dana.

"I'm here, Alecia, and I'm ready." She brandished the knife, the edge glowing red. "I'll cut as soon as the pain begins to fade. You must tell me."

"Soon, Dana," Alecia panted. "Soon." She breathed short puffing breaths, feeling the agony begin to recede. "Now."

Dana exposed her belly and ran her hand across the muscles she would soon cut. Thom turned his face away, his hands pressing against Alecia's shoulders. She lay her head against the pillow, ready for the sharp stab of hot knife across her abdomen. Soon now, soon. She closed her eyes and spoke a quick prayer to the Goddess for the strength to endure what must be endured.

A blast of cold air struck her as the bedroom door flew open and slammed against the wall. Ramón stood in the doorway, and a shaggy man with dark hair loomed behind him.

"Vard! You came." She'd know those eyes anywhere.

Vard swept Thom Andra from the bed and perched there, his ragged clothes leaving grit on the bedspread. "What do you do?" he asked, glaring at Dana. He laid his hands on Alecia's belly and she felt the child leap within her. "Take that knife away. It's not time yet."

"It's past time," Dana hissed as she watched Vard run his hands all over Alecia's abdomen. "Stupid man, we'll lose both of them if we don't act now."

Alecia watched him closely, his eyes closed as he felt over her. With each touch the babe leapt, as if he felt his father and wanted to know him.

"The babe moves," she panted. Agony ripped through her as the hands of her beloved roved over her stomach. She screamed and Dana stood, trying to pull his arms away.

"What are you doing?" Dana said, brandishing the knife at Vard.

Alecia could not believe this was happening now, when all that mattered was the babe. She gasped as Vard plucked the knife from Dana's hand and hurled it into the window frame. Thom pulled his wife away to the safety of the corner of the room, but Ramón stepped up to Alecia's side and put his hand on Vard's shoulder.

"Do you know what you're doing, man?" he asked.

Vard's hands had stilled on her lower abdomen and Alecia cried out as the babe surged upward. She screamed one last desperate primeval sound, and all went black.

* * *

What have I done? Vard removed his hands from Alecia's abdomen but the violent movements continued as though a giant snake writhed within. He reached out and touched her throat. Her pulse beat a faint, fast rhythm but she was alive. His gaze locked back onto the rounded belly before him. Horror that he might have pushed Alecia over the precipice into death froze him.

Her stomach continued to move for long moments, the only sound the heavy breathing of the people in the room. Alecia he couldn't hear at all, her face pale as a sheet and her hands cold to touch. He reached for both of her hands, rubbing them together between his for warmth.

"Come back to us, my darling. Our child needs both of us, the love of the two people who made her. She is ready to be born."

Alecia's unborn child gave two great heaving movements and was still. Dana came forward.

"I would examine her if I might, Captain?" She looked at Ramón. "Could you wrap some bricks and place them alongside her, My Lord?"

Dana laid her hands upon Alecia's belly, feeling all over it as Vard had just done. Her eyes were wide as she completed her check. "The babe has moved. I've never seen the like of it. I would swear his head is now down and ready to be born."

She continued to stare at Vard as if he were a strange new animal.

Hope surged in his heart, tempered with fear for his love. Alecia must be close to death to be so cold and look so pale. "The babe has turned? She can now be born without harm to Alecia?"

"I didn't say that, Captain." She laid the wrapped bricks Ramón brought alongside Alecia under the blankets. "The princess is exhausted, and the pain has sent her into shock. That can kill as surely as blood loss. Keep talking to her."

Alecia let out a long groan and rocked her head from side to side.

"All is well, my darling," Vard said, chaffing her hands together. "Our babe has turned and is waiting to be born."

Alecia groaned again but her eyes remained closed.

"I need you to rouse, Alecia, and help our babe be born. Come back to me. Come back to our child."

Dana trickled some water from a cup past Alecia's pale lips. She swallowed and coughed but her head remained limp on the pillow. "She's exhausted I think, and so is her womb. Her body needs sustenance to bear this child. Warm her and keep talking to her. I'll fetch a broth that might help."

Dana left the room with her husband, but Vard only had eyes for Alecia. She was so pale, so unresponsive. "What's wrong? Why can't she hear me?"

He felt a hand on his shoulder. "She can hear you, man," Ramón said. "Just keep talking."

Vard nodded and straightened his shoulders, determined he wouldn't give up. He leant forward so his breath caressed Alecia's cheek and placed his body alongside hers, his arm across her. "I love you. I know I've wronged you but come back to me and bear our child. We'll rejoice in her life."

Alecia's head twisted from side to side and she groaned as a contraction hit her, the muscles of her belly going rock hard. But he detected no pushing to ease the passage of the child. "You must push, Alecia." He pulled her forward and sat behind her, his legs on either side, his arms wrapped around her. Fear gripped him stronger than he had ever felt. He couldn't lose her, but in this situation, he had no power, no skills to ensure success. She sagged back into him as the contraction passed, her head lolling against his left shoulder.

Dana returned and trickled a dark watery broth into Alecia's mouth. She swallowed half of it before the next contraction hit.

Dana rested her hands on Alecia's abdomen as the contraction ran its course. "That was a good strong one," she said. "If only we can beseech her to push, we'll have this babe born." Her eye fell upon the knife jutting from the window frame and a tear escaped her eye. She looked at Vard. "You turned the babe. How?"

"It wasn't me. She turned herself."

Dana frowned at him but Vard couldn't let her speculate on what she had seen. He didn't understand it himself.

"Vard?" The soft voice drew his gaze below and a pair of lilac eyes looked up at him. "I'm so tired. I can't push him out. It must be the knife."

"No, darling. The babe has turned. She is ready to be born but you must help her."

"Really? She?"

"Yes, sweetheart. With the next contraction you must push and push hard." He looked to Dana who nodded her agreement. "Can you do that for me?"

Alecia squeezed her eyes tightly shut and then looked up at him again. "I'll do it."

Dana gave her more broth as they waited, her hand upon Alecia's stomach so she could predict the next contraction.

"Now," she said. "Alecia, you're nearly there. Just a few pushes and we can greet your babe."

Vard gripped each of her hands in his own and she squeezed them as she bore down upon the child within.

Dana positioned herself between Alecia's legs. "I see the head," she said. "Another push, Alecia."

Vard closed his eyes to shut out the sight of her tortured body. He had caused this, and if she died it was his fault. She bore down again, and Dana cried out.

"The head, I can see him." She reached forward. "Next contraction you must give the biggest push of all."

Alecia sagged back against Vard, her chest heaving. "I can't do it."

"I'll help," Dana said.

Vard looked for Ramón and found him standing behind Dana, his eyes round with shock. "I never imagined…"

"If you can't be of help, I suggest you leave." The hairs on Vard's neck fairly bristled at the sight of Ramón staring at Alecia's womanly parts. He turned his attention back to Alecia as Ramón left the room.

"Vard, I don't think I have the strength to push our babe out." She craned her neck to look into his eyes, her lilac gaze slicing straight into his heart and melting the resistance he had so carefully built over the preceding months.

"All will be well, darling. You're brave and strong and I believe in you. I hope our babe will be just like you." He kissed her cheek and found it cold. He swallowed down the fear and gripped her fingers again. "When the pains come, you must push as never before, and it will be over."

She nodded and turned back to stare between her knees at Dana, who had one hand on the babe's head and the other on Alecia's belly.

"Here it comes. Push now."

Vard held his breath as Alecia bore down. "Vard," she moaned, drawing his name out in a long, tight exhalation that destroyed any lingering reservations he had about his woman. Dana pulled on the babe's head gently and the child slid onto a blanket that lay on the bed.

Alecia's head lolled against his shoulder and Vard thought his heart would stop beating at the sight of his child. His daughter. Somehow, he had known Alecia bore a daughter. His intuition had been confirmed as Dana rolled the child to her side and scooped matter from her mouth.

"Is she…?" he said, easing himself from behind Alecia and laying her back against the pillows. He didn't know what to do, torn between Alecia and the babe, his heart split in two. There were no cries. Had he been too late? No, the babe had turned and been delivered with all speed after that. She was strong and healthy and there would be a sound soon. Not like his love – Alecia's face was pale and her breath shallow.

"Alecia, love," he said. "Open your eyes." He pulled the blankets up to her chin, positioning the warmed stones closer to her body. "Alecia!"

Her eyes fluttered but he could detect no other response. "Mistress Andra, she's ill." His desperate gaze sought the farm wife who thrust the babe at him.

"She hasn't taken her first breath yet," Dana said. "Sit and place her over your knee head down and gently pat her back until she cries."

Vard's hands shook as he complied, his brain unable to register anything else but the tiny body of his daughter on his lap. He tapped her back twice with his fingertips, but nothing happened.

"Harder," Dana said. "Harder still."

Vard flinched as he delivered firm slaps to the tiny back. "It's not working." Panic seized him as it never had before. His frantic gaze locked onto Mistress Andra where she chaffed Alecia's hands and murmured to the unconscious woman.

"Swing her by the feet and smack her bottom. Allow the blanket to fall but remember she is still attached to her mother."

Vard again did as he was told, fearful the child would slip from his grasp. Her skin was velvet soft beneath his calloused fingers as he slapped her tiny bottom. It felt so wrong, but suddenly there was a small gasp and an indignant bellow escaped from the mouth of his red-faced daughter.

Vard looked up to find Mistress Andra beaming and even Alecia's eyes fluttered open at the sound of her child.

"You may wrap her again and present her to her mother," Dana said, an amused smile lifting the corners of her mouth as she watched Vard standing with his daughter swinging upside down from his fingers.

He quickly laid his daughter on the bed and wrapped her inexpertly in the blanket. She hollered anew at the experience until he laid her upon her mother's chest and Alecia spoke.

"Hello, my little babe," she said. "I've labored long to bring you into this life, and I'm so glad to see you."

Vard felt he intruded and inched away. His eyes fell upon the cord that still connected his daughter to Alecia and suddenly it was all too much. He shouldn't be here, a witness to this intensely personal time. He didn't deserve Alecia's love, or this new life she had created. He was almost at the door before Alecia's voice stopped him.

"I need you." It was barely a whisper, but it cut straight to the center of his being. He turned to find the infant suckling at Alecia's breast. Had there ever been a more perfect picture of life and love than these two, together and complete? He walked back to the bed and knelt at her side.

"I love you, Vard," she said. "We have much to discuss, but I wanted to make sure you wouldn't leave. At least not yet."

He bent and brushed his lips against hers, the brief touch still invoking that shiver of anticipation they always had. "I'll be right outside." He pressed his lips to hers again and this time she kissed him back. He pulled away before the kiss could deepen further, conscious of Mistress Andra at work near them. With a last caress, he left mother and daughter to their rest.

* * *

Alecia stared out the window of her bedroom, her babe at her breast, and a gnawing fear in her stomach. It wasn't her weakness that caused her upset, or her babe, but a nagging uncertainty about what the future might hold. Vard had returned, but behind his gold-flecked gaze lurked a wildness more acute than ever. What had befallen him during his absence? How did he feel about his child? Would he abandon her all over again?

Sunflowers bumped their huge golden petals against her windowsill and a glorious sunset lit the mountains to the west. The peace of this remote farm had been all that kept her sane these past months, but she sensed the time approaching when she'd have to leave this place and take her rightful role in society. Her exile was almost at an end, but what would that mean? She looked down upon the dark hair of her daughter and marveled at the instant love she felt for the tiny mite. She was perfect in every way, and invoked a fierce protective instinct in Alecia that made her want to ensure that no one ever hurt her. Deep sadness at her own childhood washed over her. How could her father have treated her with such lack of regard? And now he was gone, with no hope of the reconciliation she had dreamed of.

Ramón poked his head around the door. "May I enter?"

"Of course." Alecia smiled at her old friend and drew the blankets across her exposed chest. "Thank you for bringing him back." What else could she add to that? He had proven his worth in finding Vard and delivering him to her, a feat that couldn't have been easy.

"You know I'd do anything for you, Princess. What will you call her?"

"We have yet to decide."

He nodded. "What will you do now?"

"First I'll recover from the birth and acquaint myself with my daughter. After that, I don't know."

"Return to Brightcastle. Benae and I will help with your daughter. You'll live the life of a princess and your people will welcome you with open arms."

"I must speak with Vard."

Dread swept across his face. "Did you see the state he was in? That was civilized compared to the way I found him in the woods. Insanity doesn't come close to describing it." He fell silent for a time, his fists bunched tight. "I wish I'd killed him when I had the chance."

"No, you don't," she said quietly. "You could never be responsible for the death of another."

He took a step back from the bed as Vard came into the room.

"I must return to Brightcastle for the birth of Princess Benae's child," Ramón said. "I'll announce that your exile is coming to an end and you may be expected back by the end of autumn. If I haven't heard from you by then, I'll return here. I'll not mention Captain Anton."

"I can't make any promises, Ramón," Alecia said.

He looked at Vard and frowned. "Time will see to that, Princess. Just promise you'll return."

Alecia drew herself up. "You may now be Guardian of Brightcastle and a lord but you don't have the power to order when I come and go. There was never any question about my return, just to the timing. I know my responsibilities, and now I have even more reason to return. I must see that the new… administration… is acting as it should."

Ramón's jaw tensed. "That's a low blow. You must know I'd never do anything to hurt the kingdom?"

"I'm sorry," she said. "I don't mean to offend you. I just have to meet your wife and see for myself that all is well. Then perhaps I can decide my future in the kingdom. I'm sure the king will have his own beliefs about who should run Brightcastle."

Ramón drew himself up, his face becoming impassive. "So be it, Princess. I'll ready Brightcastle for your return. And you'll see that Benae and I have only acted for the good of all." He turned to Vard. "I once said I'd kill you the next time I saw you. I didn't stay true to my word and you have the princess to thank for that. If you harm her again, I can't say what will happen the next time we meet."

Vard stared at Ramón as Alecia held her breath, certain there would be trouble, but he merely gave a small bow and Ramón left with a flourish of his cloak.

"Impertinent pup!" Vard said, but Alecia thought she detected the gleam of admiration in his eyes. He turned his head to her, his gold-touched emerald gaze softening as it fell upon his daughter. "What's her name?"

"I thought we could name her together. Do you have any preferences?"

Vard frowned. "What was your mother's name?"

"Iona."

"Then let us call her that. Henceforth she will be called Princess Iona of Brightcastle."

"And Izebel shall be her second name after Izebel the warrior queen."

"Iona Izebel Zialni," he said. "It has a certain ring to it."

Alecia frowned. Why hadn't he given his daughter *his* name? Anton. "We have much to talk of, Vard. Matters weren't resolved between us when you departed. What passed in that time?"

Vard took a deep breath. "I met Leth a few days out. He challenged me. He said things I hope aren't true." He walked to the window and gazed at the reds and oranges of a magnificent sunset.

A shiver ran down Alecia's spine. "What did he say?" she asked slowly. Did she really want to know?

He turned to her. "He suggested that he'd been intimate with you."

She gasped. "It's not true, Vard. I'd never betray you."

"Leth held a certain sway over you. Are you certain that in one of those moments you didn't couple with him?"

"No. How could you ever think that? I will hear no more of it. You're my only love, the only man I've given myself to. Iona is *your* daughter."

She watched Vard blush. Did he think she didn't realize his suspicions regarding Iona's paternity? Did he think he could escape his responsibilities that simply?

"I'm sorry," he said. "It was the things Leth said, implying intimate knowledge of your body, and I wasn't in my right mind."

"Don't plead insanity, Vard. I've been true to you and you've abused me, abandoned and insulted me. What more can I expect in our future? We have a daughter to protect and to raise. Will you stand up for us or are you preparing to run again now you've swept in and saved the day?"

"I told you I wasn't worthy of you. Is it only now you're beginning to see I'm right?"

His tone was hard and uncompromising, as though he wouldn't let himself feel the insults she delivered. Looking as he did – unshaven, if a little cleaner than when he burst in after nearly six months absence – anyone would wonder at her sanity for declaring him the father. But she knew the real Vard. He was so much more than this, so much more than a feral shape-shifter, out of control and frustrated with his lot. Life hadn't been kind to either of them, and it was time to reclaim their happiness.

"I love you, Vard Anton," she said, tears welling in her eyes. "You're the love of my life and the father of my child. See your daughter." She turned Iona in her arms and the infant gazed up into her father's eyes.

He gasped. "Her eyes… they're like mine!"

Alecia studied the golden flecks in her daughter's blue eyes. "I think she's a Defender, just like her father. Is it possible?"

He laughed without amusement. "You ask me? I've never met a female Defender, but it could be possible. Perhaps one day I'll know."

"I see the doubt in your eyes. You doubt me and yourself, but she has your heritage and you must be a part of her life. She needs you."

"I wouldn't abandon her."

"You would if you believed you threatened her. But it's different now. You must stay and see this through. I won't face the lonely days again as I did during my pregnancy."

Vard returned to the bed and sat beside Alecia, holding their child. She stared deep into his eyes, believing she could read his intent.

"I love you, Alecia, and I love our child. I've faced darker days than you can imagine since we parted, days when I was sure I'd never see you again. I entered a place where nothing existed but survival. I'm frightened I could slip back into that hell. I know what you're asking but are you sure you know what will be involved? I don't want to scare you again and, more importantly, I dread hurting you and Iona."

"During the time you were absent," Alecia said, reaching for his hand, "I know you were the wolf more often than not. That form saved your life and has saved me as well. I think it's time we both accepted what you are."

"Alecia," he said, his eyes unbearably sad, "it's not just the wolf. When Ramón found me, I was insane. I was a human animal. I have no real recollection of what I did. What if I slip back into that again?"

Alecia's heart ached at the fear in his voice. "You're safe here, dearest. Forget what you are and let the peace of this farm heal you. Let's spend this time, until our return to Brightcastle, building our family. You can help Master Andra with the farm."

He smiled. "I want to believe it's that simple. Is it?"

She smiled back at him. "It really is." She ignored the voice of reason that told her Vard still needed to master his gifts, especially so when their daughter might share the talent.

"Can you forgive me, my love?" he said. "I'm ashamed of my behavior after we fled Amitania. I'll never frighten you again. You have my solemn vow that I'll only ever worship you with my body."

Alecia reached out and clutched a handful of his long dark hair, pulling his face closer. "I forgive you. I know the time with Leth confused and frustrated you." She kissed him on the lips, long dormant feelings surging to the fore. "Love me now, Vard. It has been so long."

"Nay, my darling," he said, his pupils large with need. "You need time to recover. But soon we can make a brother or sister for this beautiful girl." He caressed the glossy dark hair of his daughter's head. She watched her father with serious eyes. Alecia could only imagine the glorious challenges such a child would bring.

"I shall look forward to that," she whispered, pulling him close for another kiss. She felt the surge of emotions within her man and knew it wouldn't be many days before they would again be one.

THE END

176

GLOSSARY

Places

Kingdom of Thorius (Thor- ee- us) -the kingdom of men which encompasses the King's seat of Wildecoast and the Prince's seat of Brightcastle, along with other smaller towns

Wildecoast (Will – dee – coast) -the capital city perched on the top of a cliff overlooking the sea on the east coast of Thorius; climate is mild but windy

Brightcastle - large inland town surrounded by forests and farms, three to four days ride west of Wildecoast

Amitania (Am – it – ay – nia) or *Elvandang* (Elle – van – dang) in elvish - the deserted city north of the Usetar Mountain Range in northern Thorius; once a thriving city; disputed ownership between elves and man

Usetar Range (You – set – ar) -the mountain range running across the northern parts of Thorius

People

Lenweri (Len – weir – ee) -the elven people who are tall and elegant with black skin and pointed ears and mainly dark hair; live in mountainous forests north and west of Thorius, in places encroaching onto Kingdom lands; also known as dark elves

Sis Lenweri - the faction of dark elves that wishes to take the kingdom of Thorius back from men

Defender - a race of shapeshifters who are created to defend those in danger; they sense those in need of their help; a Defender can shift into animal form and the ability is inherited through family lines

Characters

Princess Alecia Zialni (Al – ee – sha Zee – al – nee)) - the King's niece and daughter of Prince Jiseve Zialni who rules the principality of Brightcastle and is next in line to the throne. Alecia's story begins in Princess Avenger and continues in Princess in Exile.

Vard Anton - a shapeshifting Defender; army captain of Brightcastle in Princess Avenger; holder of many secrets; his story continues in Princess in Exile

Prince Jiseve Zialni (Jiss – eve Zee – al – nee) - next in line to the throne of Thorius, younger brother of the King, a widower; father of Alecia Zialni

Lady Benae Branasar (Ben-ay Bran-a-sar) – noble lady with an estate in Tylevia; heroine of The Lady's Choice; healer; now married to Ramón Zorba

Ramón Zorba (Rah – mon Zor – bah) - Lord of Wildecoast and squire to Prince Jiseve Zialni; his family have an estate south of Wildecoast; hero of The Lady's Choice; now joint Guardian of Brightcastle with Benae

Hetty – mysterious ancient woman with magical powers; once Alecia's governess and nanny; declared a witch by Prince Jiseve and sentenced to death but rescued by Alecia

King Beniel Zialni (Ben – ee – elle Zee – al – nee) - King of Thorius; lives in Wildecoast; older brother of Jiseve Zialni and uncle of Alecia Zialni; married to Adriana

Queen Adriana - wife of the King; lives in Wildecoast; Alecia's aunt

Elinor Zorba – Ramon's twin sister; dead in childbirth

Jacques Vorasava - Lieutenant in the Brightcastle army

Lord Giornan Finus (Jor – nan Fie – nus) – recently come to Brightcastle from a neighboring kingdom; Jiseve Zialni's advisor; was betrothed to Alecia before she fled Brightcastle

Jorge Andra (George Andra) – previous squire to Prince Jiseve and close friend to Alecia; killed by mercenaries who were trying to collect money from his parents

Thom and Dana Andra – parents of Jorge Andra; farmers to the west of Brightcastle

The Barans – farmers to the northwest of Brightcastle; have a son called Roser

Izebel (Is – zee – belle) – a previous warrior queen of Thorius from centuries ago, when females could rule; Alecia's idol.

Lord Leth – mysterious sorcerer and Defender who is aiding the Sis Lenweri cause and whose home is Amitania

Frel - Vard's cousin, more like a brother

Caele Aloe – (Kale Alow); sergeant in the elven army

Tur Aloe – Caele's son and soldier in Sis Lenweri army

Ade Gyndis – corporal in the Sis Lenweri army

Gir Ensalor – sword master of the Sis Lenweri

Failora – (Fay-Laura) Lord Leth's mistress

Avorelph – (Avo – ralph) one of the Lenweri gods- previous Lenweri king and great warrior.

Elven Terms

Alen = Lord

Gir = Sergeant

Ade = Corporal

ABOUT THE AUTHOR

Bernadette Rowley is a lover of epic fantasy who is a veterinarian by day and an author by night. She is currently published in the genre of high fantasy romance with eight books, all set in her fantasy world of Thorius.

When she was a young teenager, an aunt gave her a copy of The Sword of Shannara by Terry Brooks and Bernadette has lived in various fantasy worlds ever since. It's no surprise that her chosen genre when writing romance is fantasy.

"I can see these settings so vibrantly in my mind and hope my readers can too."

But Bernadette has no desire to spoon-feed her readers by laboriously describing her fantasy settings. She would rather the reader use their own imagination.

Along with sword and sorcery, dashing heroes and stunning heroines, this author includes strong healing themes in many of her books- an element central to her everyday job.

"When I started writing the Queenmakers Saga, I never imagined my day job would force its way into my stories as it has."

And of course, there are animals, especially Bernadette's beloved horses.

Bernadette lives in Brisbane, Australia, with the four heroes in her life- her husband Michael and three grown sons.

Connect with the Author

Website: www.bernadetterowley.com
Facebook: www.facebook.com/bernadetterowleyfantasy
Twitter: www.twitter.com/bt_rowley